Cursed with a poor sense of direction and a propensity to read, **Annie Claydon** spent much of her childhood lost in books. A degree in English Literature followed by a career in computing didn't lead directly to her perfect job—writing romance for Mills & Boon—but she has no regrets in taking the scenic route. She lives in London: a city where getting lost can be a joy.

Also by Annie Claydon

Saving Baby Amy
Forbidden Night with the Duke
Healed by the Single Dad Doc
From Doctor to Princess?
Firefighter's Christmas Baby
Resisting Her English Doc

London Heroes miniseries

Falling for Her Italian Billionaire
Second Chance with the Single Mum

Discover more at millsandboon.co.uk.

FALLING FOR HER ITALIAN BILLIONAIRE

ANNIE CLAYDON

MILLS & BOON

First published in Great Britain 2019
by Mills & Boon, an imprint of HarperCollins*Publishers*
1 London Bridge Street, London, SE1 9GF

Large Print edition 2019

ISBN: 978-0-263-07862-6

MIX
Paper from
responsible sources
FSC C007454

This book is produced from independently certified FSC™ paper to ensure responsible forest management. For more information visit www.harpercollins.co.uk/green.

Printed and bound in Great Britain
by CPI Group (UK) Ltd, Croydon, CR0 4YY

CHAPTER ONE

GABRIEL DEMARCO OPENED his eyes. That seemed to be quite enough work for today, so he closed them again.

'How are you feeling?' A woman's voice flowed over him like warm honey. It was a nice voice, quiet yet firm. The kind of voice that any man should take notice of.

'I could go back to sleep.' The words slipped out before he had a chance to tell himself that sleeping probably wasn't what the voice wanted him to do. And at the moment it seemed like a siren's call, which couldn't be resisted. 'Or… I could wake up.'

It sounded as if the voice was smiling. 'Why don't you wake up? You're in hospital.'

Really? The thought didn't bother him as much as it should. He was comfortable and relaxed, as if lying on a cloud. He tried opening his eyes and light seared through his brain, making his head hurt. He'd just have to keep them closed for a while…

'Which hospital?' Not that it mattered particularly. But talking might convince the voice that he'd complied with her request.

'The Royal Westminster. You're in the private wing.'

That made sense. Someone must know who he was, and that the son of Leo DeMarco, head of one of the biggest pharmaceutical companies in Europe, could stand the cost of a night's stay in hospital. Or maybe he'd been here longer than just one night. Gabriel couldn't remember.

He flexed his fingers, running his hand across his chest and then moving his legs. Everything appeared to be working. No pain. Whatever he was in here for was probably very minor…

'Open your eyes.'

No… He didn't want to. Maybe he said as much, without knowing it, or maybe the voice just read his mind, because he felt the touch of a hand against the side of his face.

'Come on. Open your eyes.'

He couldn't resist. This time the pain wasn't so bad, because the hand was shading his face. When he turned his head in the direction of the voice, a mass of red-blonde curls and a pair of blue eyes snapped suddenly into focus. What had happened to him suddenly came a very poor second in importance to who *she* was.

'What's your name? Are you a nurse?' Stupid question. She wore a dark blue sleeveless summer dress, which seemed to be held together by a few buttons and a belt around her waist. Clearly *not* a nurse unless they'd changed the uniform from sensible to sexy.

'My name's Clara Holt. I'm not a nurse, although I'm medically trained. Your father sent me.'

His father? Since when had *he* started sending women to sit at Gabriel's bedside? The thought occurred to him that maybe his father had, for once, made a marvellous choice. She was *perfezione…molto bella…* Porcelain skin and shining gold hair. Right now, making the gorgeous Clara happy was all he wanted to do…

'Grazie.' Her lips curved into a slight smile. He'd missed out her lips, and that was unforgivable…

'You speak Italian?'

'Only a few words.'

She knew the ones that mattered. Every woman

should understand the words a man said when he called her beautiful.

Wait. How many of his thoughts had sprung to his lips by mistake, and what language had he voiced them in? The feeling that this wasn't right was beginning to nag at the edge of his consciousness. If he thought a woman beautiful, he usually had the manners to wait, and make quite sure it was the kind of compliment she wanted to hear.

Gabriel shook his head, trying to clear it, and struggled to sit up. Pain shot across his temples and he suddenly felt very nauseous. The wonderful Clara reached out, gently pushing him back down onto the pillows.

'You'll feel better in a moment, just take it slowly.'

She was an angel. Clara could take him up to her cloud any day of the week and…

No! He still wasn't thinking straight. He fought to locate a sensible question in his head, and came up with only one.

'What's the matter with me?'

This was to be expected. Gabriel was still struggling with the residual effects of the drug in his bloodstream. His impulse control was impaired, and when the feeling of well-being started to wear off he'd be experiencing the worst hang-over he'd ever had.

It was best to stick to the basic facts for the moment and leave the rest until he was a little more able to get his head around it. Gabriel was clearly not quite in control of his tongue yet, and if the most important thing on his mind was that she was beautiful, then that was just a sign that he hadn't woken up properly. The shiver that his words had produced was both unnecessary and inappropriate.

'You're going to be all right.' Clara decided to skip the part about what was wrong with him.

'*Am* I? Really?' He frowned.

'Yes, you are. You might have a headache and you probably don't remember what happened last night—'

'Yes. I have a headache. And I don't have a clue how I got here.'

'The disorientation will pass, too.'

'When…?'

'Soon. You're going to be fine.' Clara reached into her bag, taking out one of the plastic bottles she'd brought with her and cracking open the seal. 'Would you like some water?'

His gaze seemed to be following her every move. 'Yes, please…'

She opened the packet of drinking straws from her bag, putting one into the bottle and leaning over to hold it close to his mouth. His fingers closed around hers, light and caressing. His touch was just as electrifying as his words had been.

But she wasn't here to experience the delights of Gabriel DeMarco's dark gaze. If all the rumours were true, there were more than enough women who were happy to share those things with him. She had a job to do and when her boss had called her at one o'clock this morning, it had been immediately obvious that being chosen for this was an opportunity. A high-profile client, in an extremely sensitive situation.

'Take it easy. Not too much…' He was gulping the water down as fast as the straw would allow, and she pulled the bottle away from him for a moment. His fingers tightened around hers, stopping her from taking the bottle back completely.

'Thank you. May I have some more, please.'

'Slowly, this time.'

He drank again, and when the bottle was half-empty he let her take it away from him. 'You know I'm a doctor?'

'Yes, I do.' Gabriel DeMarco's file contained a lot more information than that about him.

'Then you'll know that I'll understand whatever you tell me about my medical condition.'

The facts, maybe. The hows and the whys, probably not. But he seemed to be getting more and more agitated and it was clear that he wasn't going to just rely on her and go with the flow. Clara had to think carefully, and give him the information he needed without sending him into a panic.

'You inadvertently ingested a drug last night. It's not done you any lasting harm, but you'll be feeling a little groggy for a while.'

'What drug?' Clara hesitated and he reached for the call button at the side of the bed. 'If you won't tell me…'

'All right.' The last thing she wanted was any contact with the doctors and nurses, beyond what was medically necessary. The fewer people who remembered him being here the better. 'Flunitrazepam.'

His hand moved to his face, massaging his

temples with his fingers and thumb, as if he was trying to get his brain to work.

'It's not possible to *inadvertently ingest* flunitrazepam. It's manufactured with a blue dye these days, with the specific aim of making it difficult to slip into someone's drink.' His fingers wandered to his throat as a thought seemed to occur to him.

'You have a sore throat? That's because you were given activated charcoal last night by feeding tube. Your friends, Dr and Mrs Goodman, were with you the whole time, until I arrived.' Clara tried to reassure him. The uncomfortable realisation that something had happened last night and he had no memory of it was going to dawn on him any moment now.

'I remember… I think. I was going to Grant and Sara's place for dinner. Where are they?'

'They're at home. Sleeping, I imagine, I didn't arrive here until four in the morning.'

'And what exactly is your part in this, Clara?'

He was rapidly coming to his senses. She was no longer the angel with the beautiful hair, she was someone who had to justify her presence to him. It was almost a disappointment, but in professional terms it was probably just as well.

Clara reached into her bag for the bundle of identification papers.

'I work for Gladstone and Sullivan Securities. You recognise the name...?'

'Of course. My father's company has used you for years.' He frowned suddenly. 'Please tell me I haven't done anything that requires *that* level of discretion.'

'You've done nothing wrong.' Clara handed him the documents. The answer to the question of why exactly he needed security was an awkward one and should probably wait until he was recovered enough to handle it.

He flipped open her passport, glancing at it, and then took his time reading the faxed letter of introduction. 'My father sent this at two in the morning. Clearly he thinks the situation is serious.' Gabriel came straight to the realisation that Clara was hoping he'd overlook.

'I'm sure you must know that anything connected with your well-being is considered serious.' Clara skirted the issue. 'The two most important things for you to know are who I am, and that I have the situation fully under control.'

'I'd prefer it if *I* had the situation fully under control. And since you're obviously leaving out a few important details, I think the next thing I need to do is to get out of here and find someone who *will* tell me what's going on.'

Clara's clients fell broadly into two categories. The ones who didn't want to know, and those who wanted to know everything. She generally preferred the latter, but it brought different challenges, and it was clear that Gabriel DeMarco had decided to be as challenging as possible.

'I'll be happy to tell you everything. We have a hotel suite for you nearby—'

'What's the matter with my house? Not fallen down during the night, has it?'

'No, your house is fine…'

'Good. I'm fine and so is my house.' He shot her a look that left her under no illusions that he'd believe her reassurances a little better when he had concrete proof. 'So I'm sure you won't have any objections to my going there.'

Clara took a breath. 'I'd advise—'

'No, you don't get to do that. I'm going home and if you want to accompany me and tell me exactly what's going on, you're welcome to do so. *Then* you can advise me and I'll decide whether to take that advice.'

He sat up slowly, reaching for the controls for

the bed. He must still be feeling very groggy, but that wasn't going to stop him.

'All right. I have a car outside, and we'll take you there.'

'Okay, thanks. I'll take a shower and get dressed…' He waited, obviously expecting Clara to leave the room.

'Let me help you.'

'I can manage…'

'And I'm tasked with your safety, Dr DeMarco. Letting you fall over and crack your head open on the bathroom floor isn't anywhere on my agenda.'

The thought of telling him that she doubted he had anything she hadn't already seen hundreds of times before leapt to the tip of her tongue and stopped there. The flimsy hospital gown couldn't disguise a pair of strong shoulders. Gabriel De-Marco had a good physique, made even better by dark hair and melting brown eyes in a face made proud by high cheekbones. She doubted if she'd seen *anything* quite like him before.

He smiled slowly. 'That's a bit more like it. We'll get along far better if you're straight with me. And while you're about it, call me Gabriel. I have a feeling that knowing more about my last sixteen hours than I do justifies first names.'

'Very well.' Clara opened the small wardrobe behind her chair and took out a hospital dressing gown. Gabriel operated the controls on the bed, getting to his feet slowly and pulling the dressing gown on, tying it firmly at the waist. He took a couple of steps and then waved her away.

'Good enough for you?'

'No, you look a little unsteady.' If he wanted honesty, that was exactly what she'd give him.

'How's this, then?' He walked across the room, obviously making an effort to pull himself out of the cloying arms of the drug. 'While you're giving me a little privacy you can go and ask the doctor if he can prescribe something for this headache.'

He rattled off a list of painkillers and anti-emetics. He must feel pretty awful.

'Or I could tell him that you have a headache and that you feel sick, and see what he suggests.' Most doctors didn't much like their patients telling them what to prescribe.

'I'll leave you to phrase the request tactfully.' He gave Clara a brisk farewell nod, which indicated that her next move was to leave the room and close the door behind her.

When he'd been lying down, Gabriel's main concern had been to get Clara out of the room before he asked her into the shower with him to scrub his back. He felt a lot more in control of himself now, but it was impossible to tell whether the effects of the flunitrazepam might loosen his tongue again. Or the effects of Clara Holt's dazzling blue eyes.

As soon as he was on his feet, though, another reason for wanting to be alone asserted itself. The pounding in his head became almost unbearable, and as soon as the door closed behind her, he rushed into the bathroom. His stomach was empty but still it twisted into knots as he fell to his knees, retching violently.

Shaking, and covered in a cold sweat, he got to his feet, flushing away the evidence. Gabriel rinsed his mouth, trying to get rid of the taste left by the charcoal, and looked at his reflection in the mirror. Why did he have to meet the most beautiful woman he'd ever seen today, of all days?

But Clara Holt wasn't just a beautiful woman.

She had the answer to a number of key questions. He'd take this slow and steady. One thing at a time. And the first thing was to have a shower and get dressed.

He didn't remember selecting the clothes that were folded neatly on a chair, and was reasonably sure he wouldn't have put that shirt with those trousers. Perhaps Grant and Sara had been back to his house, they had a spare key. Yet another question.

When he opened the door to his room, Clara was standing right outside it, holding a clipboard and the medication he'd asked for. She took advantage of his instinctive move to stand aside for her, and walked back into the room, closing the door behind her.

'You're looking better.' Her smile was kind, but just enough to let him know that she was happy with the way things were going, rather than giving any indication that she was here for her own pleasure.

'Thank you. It's good of you to say so.' Gabriel sat down on the bed, picking up the half-bottle of water that Clara had left on the table, and she tipped the tablets from the dispenser into his hand.

'I'll be better when these kick in. And when I get home.' If Clara had any thoughts of taking him anywhere else, she could think again. Gabriel had an almost irrational longing to be able to shut his front door behind him and come to terms with all of this.

'You'll be needing these.' She reached into her handbag, which was large enough to contain all manner of things and probably did, and produced his keys and his wallet.

'Thanks. You have my phone?'

'Your father gave us permission to send it to our labs and get it checked over for any… intrusions.'

Gabriel rolled his eyes, regretting the movement almost immediately as pain shot through his temples. 'And how long did my father say you could keep it?'

'I'll make sure you have it back tomorrow morning.' She had the grace to sound a little embarrassed about it.

He'd argue that one out later. And since Clara was obviously acting on instructions, he'd take the less inviting option of sorting the matter out with his father, and not her.

'Okay, fair enough. Can we go now?'

Clara nodded. 'Yes. Ian Anderson's outside. I think you know him.'

'Yes, I know him.' Ian drove his father when he was in London, and Gabriel knew and liked him. It seemed that Clara had done her homework and was making a comprehensive effort to reassure him. 'Is a doctor available to discharge me?'

'No need for that. You can leave whenever you feel up to it, you just need to sign this form.' She put the clipboard on the bed beside him.

He read the form. Advice on possible complications after ingesting drugs…he knew that. Counselling and other follow-up…he'd take that under advisement. Clara handed him a pen and he scribbled his name at the bottom of the form.

'Is that it?' This was far more straightforward than usual, even for a private facility.

'Yes, that's it. Are you ready?'

He was more than ready. He followed Clara out of the room, nodding to Ian, who fell into step behind them. She handed the clipboard to a nurse at the reception desk, who gave him a smile before Clara hurried him away. Outside, an SUV with tinted windows drew up, and Ian opened the back door, waiting for Gabriel and Clara to climb in, before he rounded the car and got into the front passenger seat.

They were well organised, he had to give them that. But the overwhelming probability was that this was all some kind of mistake, and that his father had done the expected and overreacted. Gabriel closed his eyes, leaning back on the leather seat, as the car drew away.

'I assume the bill's paid. I'd hate to think we were doing a runner.' He decided that teasing her a little couldn't hurt, and it made all of this seem a bit more normal.

'Yes, we've paid.' Her voice betrayed a hint of humour. 'It'll be itemised on your account when you receive it.'

'Good. And who did you tell them you were? Mata Hari?' In truth she didn't have the air of a femme fatale, although she could probably pull the look off without any trouble at all. But his father's protection officers generally blended into the background, only betraying their presence when needed. In her summer dress and low heels, Clara could easily have passed for a concerned girlfriend. A very attractive one at that.

'I said I was a friend.'

'One who's armed and dangerous?' Gabriel opened his eyes. The accompanying pain in his head was a small price for taking another look at her.

'No. Carrying a concealed weapon would be illegal.' She gave him a bright smile. 'I can be dangerous, though, if I put my mind to it.'

He'd take a bet on it. Gabriel was under no illusions that Clara Holt's smile could be extremely dangerous, even if she didn't go to the trouble of putting her mind to it.

CHAPTER TWO

GABRIEL HAD BEEN silent for the rest of the drive back to his house. When they drew up outside the three-storey town house, situated in one of London's most exclusive Georgian terraces, Gabriel moved to get out of the car, and Clara stopped him, laying her hand on his arm.

'I'd like you to stay here for a moment while Ian and the other members of my team check the house.' She indicated the car parked across the street, containing four more security officers. 'Is that okay?'

She felt the muscles of his arm flex under her fingers as his hand clenched into a fist. Then Gabriel puffed out a breath, reaching for his keys and handing them to Ian. 'All right. When we *do* get inside you'll have some questions to answer...'

Clara knew that. Ian flashed her the briefest of looks, which said that he wouldn't want to be in her shoes, and got out of the car.

Her team knew what they were doing, and they didn't have to wait long before an all-clear was signalled to Clara. Gabriel was stony-faced as she accompanied him up the front steps and through the panelled front door into a large, bright hallway.

'You'll join me for a cup of tea.' That didn't sound like an invitation but an order. Clara followed him through to the kitchen.

The room was obviously designed with some serious cooking in mind. A large double hob with pans of all shapes and sizes hanging to one side, all of them well used. An array of herbs and spices was contained in a rack full of jars, and a wine cooler was well stocked with bottles. At the far end, a breakfast table stood in a semicircular bay and Gabriel strode towards it, drawing the blinds against the sunlight that streamed in through the French doors. Turning to inspect the supermarket bag that her team had left on the counter, he raised an eyebrow.

'What's this?'

'Since we don't know where the flunitrazepam came from, it's wise to view your existing food stocks as suspect for the time being.'

He shook his head, taking teabags and milk

from the bag and making the tea. When he put the two mugs on the table, sitting down opposite her, she found herself shivering in the heat of his dark gaze.

'There's one thing I want to get straight.'

'Of course.'

'You're managing me. You're very good at it, and I appreciate that you might find it necessary in a lot of the situations that you encounter, but I want you to stop.'

Clara swallowed hard. His file hadn't prepared her for this. Gabriel DeMarco was the son of a man who was so rich that most people couldn't get their heads around the scale of his wealth. Gabriel ran a medical charity, which no doubt gave him the sense that he was doing something useful, and the rest of the time he did what he pleased. He was undoubtedly charming, and the file had hinted that he used his not inconsiderable talent for seduction on a regular basis. Nothing...nothing had prepared her for his incisive mind and his determination.

But she could adapt. 'Yes, I am managing you. This is a...sensitive situation.'

'I understand that. But if we're to have any

kind of relationship, I want all the facts. Even the ones you think I can't handle.'

'Very well. I'll tell you everything.'

'Good.' Gabriel leaned back in his seat, rubbing his temples. 'Go on, then…'

Clara puffed out a breath. This felt like some kind of test, and she was pretty sure that if she left anything out now, she was going to fail it.

'Yesterday evening you went to Dr and Mrs Goodman's house for dinner. You collapsed shortly after you arrived. Dr Goodman recognised your symptoms as being drug related and took the appropriate action.'

'And what prompted your involvement?'

'Mrs Goodman knows your father, I believe.'

Gabriel rolled his eyes. 'Yes, they've stayed with us in Italy. Sara called him, didn't she?'

'Yes, she did, and that turned out to have been a very wise move. It appears there have been other incidents involving your family…'

His brow darkened suddenly. 'Other incidents? Is my mother all right?'

'Your mother's fine, nothing's been directed at her. Although she's naturally concerned about you, and we've been in constant contact with your parents to put their minds at rest.'

'Thank you.' His gaze was searching her face. 'You should know that my older brother died in an accident when he was seventeen. My mother wouldn't be human if she didn't worry a little too much about me sometimes.'

'Mr Sullivan told me. I was chosen for this assignment because I can be tactful and discreet. And I know how to reassure the people I work with.'

'In that case, I'd be grateful if you could employ your ability to reassure to its fullest extent when you deal with my parents.'

'But not with you?'

'No. Not with me.' Lines of worry and exhaustion etched themselves on his face, and for a moment all Clara wanted to do was soothe them away. 'Why would anyone want to do this? I can't imagine you don't have a theory.'

'You must know about the new drug your father's company has developed.' Maybe he didn't. Maybe he just took the money and didn't take much interest in the way it was made.

'Yes, of course I do. It's one of the new generation of HIV drugs and because of the low cost of manufacture it has huge potential in developing countries.' Gabriel frowned. 'I know that there have been some questions in the press about our manufacturing capabilities and distribution policies. When a new drug is developed, everyone else wants to get their hands on it and it's not unusual to find a bit of pressure being applied to the company that holds the rights.'

'Well, it may be that someone's taken that application of pressure a step further. There have been moves to put your father under investigation for financial irregularities…'

'What?' Gabriel gave a harsh laugh. 'I hadn't heard about that, but whoever suggested it doesn't know him very well. My father's an absolute stickler for things being done properly as far as money's concerned.'

'So I gather. But you must know that getting the relevant distribution licences for a drug with this much potential is a demanding process. Any hint of scandal has to be avoided, and since it's common knowledge that you'll be having a greater involvement with the company when your father retires, that extends to you.'

Gabriel thought for a moment. 'Okay… I get the financial allegations, they're a direct attack on the company's suitability to develop an important drug properly. The PR department will deal with that. But I don't see the connection between that and what's happened to me.'

'Timing...' Clara counted out her points on her fingers. 'Ingestion of a form of flunitrazepam that isn't available on the open market... Mrs Goodman's emphatic assertion that you're not a drug user...correct me if she's wrong about that.'

'Sara's right. I don't touch drugs.'

He was quiet for a moment, his face grave. Clara could almost see his life crumbling around him, and the thought that she'd been the one to tell him all of this made her feel sick.

'I'm sorry, Gabriel. This can't be easy to hear.'

'That's all right. I appreciate your honesty.' He looked up at her, and suddenly she was on unsteady ground, falling into the warmth of his dark eyes. 'Look, I really need to sleep for a few hours. Can I give you a call this afternoon, and we'll talk a bit more?'

The after-effects of the drug were hitting him hard. Gabriel had kept it together for longer than most would have done, but now he could hardly keep his eyes open.

'I'll stay here, with my team.'

He looked around, as if he'd forgotten that they weren't alone in the house. That was exactly what Clara wanted. Her team did their jobs quietly and inconspicuously and a client didn't need to know the nuts and bolts of it. All Gabriel needed to know was that they were there and he was safe.

'Uh… Okay. Help yourself to…' He gestured towards the fridge and then seemed to think better of it and shrugged.

This was how it started. Gabriel was the kind of man who was sure of his place in the world, but gradually he was beginning to question the safety of everything around him. Clara had seen it happen before, and knew that it would be a difficult challenge for him to face.

'Take some water with you.' She got to her feet, pulling a bottle of water from the supermarket bag and giving it to him. 'I have to call your father to give him an update. Or would you prefer to do that?'

Gabriel shook his head, wincing in sudden pain. 'No. This is a company matter, he'll want a report from you, not me. Tell him I said hello if you like, and that I'll call him later.'

He turned, walking slowly out of the room. Clara saw his hand shake as he reached for the door handle and wondered if he'd make it up the stairs on his own. But instinct told her that crowding him would be the wrong thing to do at the moment, so she listened for his unsteady footsteps, relaxing only when she heard the sound of a door closing upstairs.

She'd watched over Gabriel's handsome, sleeping face since the early hours of this morning. Stared at it, unable to believe that anyone could look quite so perfect…

But now wasn't the time to think about his perfections. It was the vulnerabilities that she had to deal with, the worries and the flaws that came out when a person was in a difficult situation and under pressure. And although Gabriel wasn't ready to admit it yet, he *was* in a very difficult situation.

CHAPTER THREE

ALONE IN HIS bedroom Gabriel tore off his clothes, leaving them in an untidy pile on the floor, and threw himself down on the bed. The room was bathed in sunlight and it was hurting his eyes so he reluctantly got up again and drew the curtains. That was better.

He was so tired. Asleep almost before he lay back down…

Eleven years old and alone in the darkness. His leg hurt. Gabriel had dragged himself over to the heap of rocks that had fallen near the mouth of the cave and tried desperately to move them, but they were too big. He'd called his brother's name, knowing that he wouldn't answer but hoping somehow for a miracle. Pietro had been buried, along with his friends, and only Gabriel was left.

Time was measured only by fitful sleep and growing hunger pains.

He heard the sound of water, and crawled to find it, pain shooting through his injured leg. The water tasted clean and cool, marred only by the metallic taste of his own blood, where he'd torn his fingers trying to dig.

He lay down on the floor of the cave. It would be better if he stayed here. Pietro was here, and his ghost seemed to beckon Gabriel into his arms...

Gabriel woke with a start, cold sweat covering his body. *Breathe. Wake up.* He commanded himself back into the world of the living. Rolling off the bed and stumbling to the bathroom, he turned on the tap, immersing his face in cold water, the shock bringing him to his senses.

Sometimes he'd go for weeks without having the dream. Then something would happen and it would be back again, never changing and still so real that he could almost touch it. Gabriel supposed that the sedative effects of the flunitrazepam might have something to do with it this time. Or maybe the feeling that he was trapped now too, with unknown dangers surrounding him.

He didn't remember the rescuers bringing him

out of the cave, he'd been too far gone by then, but he remembered waking up with his mother at his bedside. He'd seen the light streaming in through the windows, and promised himself he'd never be trapped again. He'd stay in the light and the fresh air, and he'd go wherever he wanted, whenever he wanted.

His parents' constant, and understandable, concern for him had made that promise difficult to fulfil during the uneasy years of his teens. But Gabriel had learned to keep the peace, giving his mother the reassurance she needed while still reserving a measure of freedom for himself.

Gabriel switched on the shower, soaping himself clean, trying to tease his mind away from the dregs of the nightmare. He should concentrate on all the bright things his life contained. The memory of Clara's cool fingers on his face suddenly burst into his head, making him shiver.

He wondered vaguely what Clara would have to say about the freedom that he valued so greatly. The thought that she had no authority to say *anything* about the way he led his life was tempered by the idea that it was probably her reports to his parents that were keeping his mother sane at the moment. And the growing realisation that he liked her. She was honest, and she had the kind of strength that he admired in a person.

And she was beautiful. Maybe it was his drugged state that had endowed her with the most beautiful face he'd ever seen. The fantasy of being approached by a gorgeous woman and told he was in danger from a criminal plot seemed like something out of a spy thriller.

Wrapping a towel around his waist, he padded back into the bedroom, glancing at the clock. It was already three in the afternoon, and he'd slept too long. He should go downstairs and face Clara. Then maybe this whole situation, and Clara herself, would seem a little more ordinary.

'Still here, then.' Clara had heard Gabriel moving around upstairs for the last half-hour. When he appeared in the kitchen doorway he had showered and shaved, and looked a great deal better than he had first thing this morning.

She looked up at him and gave him a smile. 'You thought I was going somewhere?'

He shrugged. 'I wasn't entirely sure that you were ever here at all. I suppose that what you said this morning still stands as well?'

'Yes. I'm afraid it does.' Disbelief was a common enough reaction. But the smiling, casual joke that Gabriel made of it was unusual. Most people were a bit more visceral about it, almost pleading with her to tell them that it was all a mistake.

'Since this all seems to be real…my first concern is for the well-being of my charity. I assume you have details of The Watchlight Trust.' He nodded towards the laptop that was open in front of her on the kitchen table.

In the circumstances, his first concern should be for his life. Maybe Gabriel took it for granted that he was invulnerable, the rich frequently did. But it seemed she'd found something that he cared about enough to want to protect it.

'Yes, I do. Interesting name…'

'We aim to serve those who keep a watchlight burning and are there for us when we're in trouble.'

'I can support that. I used to work as an ambulance paramedic…' Clara bit her tongue. Her own past wasn't relevant here.

But it was too late. His gaze had caught hers and there was no escape. 'You know, it seems a little unfair that you know all about me and I know so little about you.'

He'd laid a trap for her and she'd fallen straight into it. Clara felt her cheeks redden. 'You can have a copy of my CV…'

He shot her a languid smile. 'Don't do that. I prefer a more personal approach to information-gathering.'

For now, getting the file straight was Clara's primary focus, and the idea of a personal approach was disconcerting. She cleared her throat. 'And what exactly does The Watchlight Trust do?'

'We're building a knowledge and research base, and we run courses and conferences for people in the emergency and other rescue services. Alistair Duvall and I co-founded the charity five years ago. We're both medical doctors with training in traumatic injury. Alistair specialises in physical rehab and limb replacement, and my speciality is in PTSD and its associated disorders. We run a clinic, next door to our offices, which deals mainly with outpatients but we do have facilities for fifteen in-patients as well.'

'And the clinic is solely for rescue service personnel?'

Gabriel shook his head. 'Not now. We came to the very obvious realisation that the techniques we were using to help those who were injured while rescuing others could be applied across a wider range of people. We welcome anyone who feels we can help them.'

He grinned suddenly, waiting for her to finish typing the extra information into the file on her laptop. 'Got all that, or do you want me to go a bit slower?'

'I'm keeping up. Could someone damage your own reputation or that of DeMarco Pharmaceuticals by attacking The Watchlight Trust?'

'If anyone attacks The Watchlight Trust then my reputation is the least of my worries.' The gleam of defiance in his eyes might be commendable, but it wasn't going to help with the security situation. 'Legally speaking and in terms of culture and decision-making, the charity is entirely separate from my father's company.'

'And in practice?'

Gabriel puffed out a breath. 'In practice, DeMarco Pharmaceuticals lends us conference and training facilities from time to time, and we have use of the private plane when it's available. My mother throws a fundraiser every year, which brings in a lot of money. And although I'm nominally a salaried director, I don't draw my salary because I have an allowance from the family trust.'

'And do you put any of your own money into the charity?'

'There are a few high-risk projects that I fund myself, on the basis that they're largely a gamble.' She noted the gleam in his eyes as he spoke. Apparently *high risk* was something that excited him, and that was going to be a concern.

She'd deal with that later. 'So in terms of public perception, The Watchlight Trust has a very great deal to do with DeMarco Pharmaceuticals. I think we must consider security at their offices.'

He nodded. 'That sounds wise. Alistair's the one to contact about that, you have his number?'

Clara nodded. 'I have a proposal for CCTV and movement sensors that we can install here in your house, too…'

'No.' He turned and flipped open a cupboard, raising one eyebrow when he found it empty. 'You've been busy. What did you do with the teabags?'

'Next cupboard along.' Gabriel clearly wasn't inclined to discuss the need to send everything in his kitchen off for testing, any more than he wanted to discuss CCTV. But Clara had to take measures to ensure his safety.

'Security cameras aren't designed to invade your privacy. We can position them discreetly and you'll forget they're even there…'

He put teabags into two mugs, setting the kettle to boil. Then turned, leaning against the countertop, his arms folded. 'I'll save you the trouble. I don't want any kind of surveillance equipment in my house.'

This was her way in. 'Then you'll be pleased to hear that we've swept the house for bugs, and didn't find anything.'

A pulse started to beat at the side of his forehead. Gabriel was obviously coming to the realisation that Clara wasn't the only one who might be watching or listening. It didn't seem to please him.

'What makes you think that you would?'

'Have you worked out how the flunitrazepam got into your system yet?'

His gaze left her face and Gabriel stared pensively at the floor. 'No.'

'Neither have I. Until we do, we need to assume that anything's possible.'

'Or maybe we should try not to jump to conclusions, and assume that things are okay until we know otherwise.'

'And what would you consider a reliable warning that things *aren't* okay? You ending up in hospital?' Clara pressed her lips together. That point would have been better made calmly.

'I don't have an answer to that.' Gabriel looked up at her, the knowingness in his eyes making her shiver. He seemed to see straight through her, past her veil of professionalism and right down to the moment when seeing him lying in that hospital bed had made her want to reach out and touch him.

'Neither do I. But we'll know more tomorrow, and until then I need to assume the worst. Which means that the only alternative to CCTV is that I stay here in the house tonight, with a full protection detail.'

Oddly enough, that didn't seem to bother Gabriel too much. Maybe he'd come to the conclusion that, however good her team was, they couldn't see through closed doors. 'I'm always happy to have house guests. I have to make some phone calls and then I'll make the spare room up for you.'

He'd be infuriating if it weren't for that charm of his. Actually, he *was* infuriating, but the charm made it all too easy to forgive him.

'The spare room won't be necessary.' Clara could catch a few hours in a chair, she'd slept in worse places. 'And if you want to make any calls, would you use my phone? I'm still waiting to hear back about the checks on your landline.'

She slid the phone across the table and Gabriel nodded, turning to pour the tea. He put one cup down on the table in front of her, then picked up her phone and strode out of the kitchen.

She could handle this. She wasn't going to mess up. Clara twisted her fingers together in her lap and took a breath. This was the chance she'd been waiting for, a make-or-break career move, looking after one of Gladstone and Sullivan Securities' most valued clients. She couldn't allow herself to lose focus.

She'd already come so far. Her parents' divorce had turned her life into a constant trek between her mother's and father's houses, as both of them warred over custody and pretty much everything else. Clara had escaped that and made a home for herself. And then her life had collapsed around her again. When she was tempted to see only Gabriel's handsome face and his smile, she should remember why she'd promised herself she would never be taken in by a man again.

Six in the morning, and she'd travelled all night so she could surprise her husband. After an eleven-month tour of duty as a paramedic with the Army Reserve, Clara had arrived home.

Tim would still be sleeping and she took her boots off and climbed the stairs silently. The Clara who had trusted reached out her hand and opened the bedroom door.

She could still feel the tearing pain as she'd seen Tim, sleeping peacefully in the light of early dawn, his arm around a woman Clara had called her friend. It had been at that precise moment that trust had become a thing of the past.

She'd run down the stairs, hearing shocked voices as Tim and Sandra had woken suddenly. Picking up her boots and bag, she'd been gone before Tim had been able to follow her, slamming the front door behind her. Out into a world where her marriage was in ruins and she had nowhere to call home.

* * *

That had been four years ago. Clara had taken that moment and let it drive her. She'd worked hard, calculating every move she made. No more moments of shocked betrayal. And a home that she could truly call her own that no one could take away.

She had a good job and a nice flat. She relied on herself, and there was no way that Gabriel's smile was going to tempt her into risking all of that.

Gabriel retreated to his study, sprawling on the sofa. Resisting the impulse to access Clara's photographs to see if there were pictures of dogs or children or anything else that might betray that she had a life beyond this, he flipped through the contacts. His father's number was there, along with Sara's mobile number and the main number of his charity.

The first call was the easiest. Sara and Grant brushed off his apologies, wanting only to know whether he was all right. The second was a little more taxing. Gabriel's co-director at The Watchlight Trust, Alistair Duvall, had not been satisfied with blanket reassurances and had questioned him more closely. Then Gabriel called his father.

He lay on the sofa, studying the ceiling as his father swung into employer mode and issued instructions. This was a serious matter, and he knew that Gabriel shared his concern that the company should not be compromised. He was to follow the advice of his security team at all times. Gabriel mouthed the words of his parting shot, knowing them off by heart. He wasn't to worry his mother. She'd already lost one son…

He knew. He'd been there. The last twenty years had been dedicated to not worrying his mother, and to trying to make up for the son that his parents had lost. To stepping into the shoes of the older brother he'd hero-worshipped. Gabriel did what he always did, assuring his father that he'd heard, and asking to speak to his mother.

That was a less demanding conversation. His mother's fears could be assuaged by the sound of his voice, and the promise that he was fine, if a little groggy still. They chatted for a while, and when he was sure that his mother was content, Gabriel ended the call.

He closed his eyes, stretching his limbs, wondering whether it was time to take more painkillers. Perhaps he should ask Clara, she seemed to have pretty much every area of his life under control.

But tomorrow he'd take it all back. Tomorrow was a new day. One more day that his brother didn't have, and Gabriel had promised himself a long time ago that he'd waste none of them.

CHAPTER FOUR

CLARA OPENED HER EYES. This was a nice place to wake up, quiet, early morning sunlight filtering into the large guest bedroom. Maybe it was the lingering strands of a dream that made her feel that Gabriel had somehow only just left the room.

Gabriel had insisted she get a night's sleep, and Clara had been too tired to argue. This morning she had to concede that he'd been right. She felt rested and equal to the task of finding a way to reconcile Gabriel's urge to do whatever he pleased, whenever he pleased, with a workable security protocol.

She showered and dressed quickly, shaking the creases out of the smart trousers and blouse that she kept in the overnight bag in the boot of her car. There were guards stationed inside and outside the house, but it wouldn't do any harm to take an early morning tour to make sure that everything was as it should be.

'He's up.' Molly, one of the night guards, was at her post in the front hallway, and frowning furiously. 'He's been out…'

'You went with him?' Clara raised her eyebrows.

'No, he must have slipped out through the back somehow. Walked back in through the front door. Sorry, Clara.'

Clara shook her head. 'It's not your fault. Where is he now?'

'Kitchen.'

'Okay. Thanks, Molly.' Clara turned, taking a breath as she walked towards the closed kitchen door. If Gabriel was starting as he meant to go on, then so was she.

He was sitting at the kitchen table, a takeaway coffee and pastry in front of him. Reading the paper. He wore a crisp white shirt with a tie, and dark trousers, and his demeanour suggested that butter wouldn't melt in his mouth. Clara brushed away the thought that his mouth was probably capable of turning solid rock into molten lava.

'Morning.' He gave her a smile, and Clara sat down at the table. 'Would you like some coffee?'

Clara shook her head. 'You've been out to get yours?'

'I can't drink instant.' He nodded to the jar of coffee that had been bought to replenish his empty cupboards yesterday.

'So you decided to take a stroll and get some. Along with a morning paper.'

'I brought coffee back for the night guards as well. I was going to get some for you, but I didn't want to wake you.'

His charm was working overtime. Liquid brown eyes that seemed to collude with her and invited her to collude with him.

'You can't do this, Gabriel.'

'I just have.' He shot her a penetrating look. 'You're not my keeper, Clara.'

The words rolled off his tongue so easily, as if he'd come to the conclusion that no one was his keeper a long time ago. They'd be sure to hurt anyone who cared about him…

Clara placed her palms on the table in front of her, leaning forward. 'I *am* your keeper, because that's what I'm paid to be. And if you think that bringing everyone coffee is going to make any difference, when you've just gone out of your way to demonstrate that my team can't do their jobs properly, then you're wrong.'

She was taking a risk. But Gabriel wasn't going

to terminate the contract and order her out of the house. Even if he didn't care to acknowledge the risks he was facing, he obviously cared about his mother and wouldn't do anything to worry her.

'It wasn't the night guards' fault. I take full responsibility…' A flicker of genuine remorse showed in his face.

'That's not how it works, Gabriel. If some harm had come to you, they would have been held responsible. I won't have them treated like that.'

'All right. I hear you, and I apologise. But I won't make this house into a fortress that I'm afraid to leave. It's like…being buried alive.'

Gabriel seemed suddenly hollow-eyed at the prospect. He *had* been buried alive. The details in his file were scanty, but basic facts had been noted. The accident that had killed his brother had trapped him underground for three days.

'I hear you, too.' She could feel his pain, hanging in the air between them and pounding in her chest. 'If you'll work with me, I'll respect your wishes. Always and without question.'

Suddenly he capitulated. 'All right. I'd like to go in to the charity's offices this morning, there are a few things I need to discuss with Alistair. If you can facilitate that, I'd be grateful.'

Clara nodded, puffing out a breath. 'Thank you. We'll be ready to go when you are.'

'Half an hour? I'll make you some coffee. Instant, I'm afraid…'

He'd made a concession and now wasn't the time to tell him that coffee was the last thing on her mind. 'Thank you. I'll go and tell the guards and be back in a moment.'

Clara had seen Gabriel approach each one of the night guards before they went off duty, and had heard his apology. He'd thanked them for their night's work and shaken their hands. It wasn't necessary, they were all used to being treated like part of the furniture, but it was a nice thing for him to do and everyone appreciated it.

She'd also seen the words that Molly had mouthed to Ian when she handed over to him. *He's so hot…* Ian had delivered a smiling reproof. That wasn't something that anyone needed to notice, and Clara should take the advice on board too.

The charity's offices were just ten minutes' drive away. Quietly exclusive, the three-storey building looked out on a leafy square, bounded by iron railings. Gabriel waited until Ian opened the door of the SUV for him and followed him up the front steps. Once inside, he seemed to regain his momentum, giving the guard in Reception a brisk wave and striding through into an open-plan studio.

'These are our main offices, and we have a development team upstairs, along with a meeting room. Our clinic is next door, and it also takes up the top floor of this building.'

Clara knew that already. She'd seen the schematics for the two buildings. But Gabriel seemed to be intent on co-operation and she wasn't going to discourage him.

'Thanks. That's useful to know.'

He gestured towards a couple of glass-walled offices at the far end of the main space, one of which was occupied by a man who had sprung to his feet when they entered.

'That's my office and Alistair's is next door…' He broke off, greeting the man with a smile. 'Alistair. This is Clara Holt. She's closer to me than my shadow at the moment.'

That was the aim. When she could keep up with him.

'Nice to meet you, Clara.' Alistair gave her a relaxed grin, and Gabriel hurried away, towards his own office. 'We need to talk, Gabriel…' he called after him.

'Yes, we do. Be with you in a minute.' Gabriel was sorting through the papers on his desk, obviously trying to find something.

'Don't let him run rings around you.' Gabriel's habit of doing the exact opposite of whatever he was meant to be doing clearly came as no surprise to Alistair. 'Thanks for sending your colleague in to see us yesterday, by the way. It was a really useful session, and it's good to know we're bug-free.'

'Thank you for being so…co-operative.'

Alistair chuckled. 'My pleasure entirely. You'll find that Gabriel can be co-operative if he puts his mind to it.'

Clara would wait and see about that. And meanwhile she'd watch and learn. It seemed that the two directors were a fusion of opposites, and if Alistair could get him to co-operate then there was hope for her.

He turned as Gabriel shot back out of his office, making towards them. 'Clara, feel free to use my desk, we won't be long. Ready, Alistair?'

'I have been for the last ten minutes.' Alistair began to follow Gabriel towards his own office and then turned to Clara. 'We actually might be a while. Refreshments are over there.'

The guards outside would be making sure that no one who wasn't supposed to be here would be finding their way past the reception area and Clara could watch and learn. She found a seat that gave an unobstructed view of both Gabriel and Alistair through the glass wall that divided the two offices. Alistair sat back in one of the easy chairs to one side of his desk, obviously listening. Gabriel was more animated. The conversation seemed to be getting heated and Gabriel rose and paced a little, then threw himself back into his seat.

It was clearly a case of an irresistible force meeting an unmovable object. Just as Clara was wondering whether there would inevitably be an explosion of some sort, and whether it might be wise to take cover, Gabriel smiled and Alistair nodded. Peace was restored, only to be shattered again when they started in on a new topic of discussion.

Sitting and watching. Waiting for nothing to happen and yet prepared for anything. Clara had become used to it, but Gabriel made it a lot less tedious. Something about the way he moved invited her to watch, and it was difficult to tear her gaze away from him and scan the office, as people filtered in to start their day's work. Names would have been checked at Reception and her presence seemed to excite a studied lack of interest. Alistair had clearly already dealt with any questions about the situation.

After two hours, it seemed that Gabriel and Alistair had run out of things to wrangle about and it looked as if neither of them could be any more pleased about the outcome of their discussions. Gabriel picked up the sheaf of papers he'd brought with him, tucking them under his arm, and joined Clara in his own office.

'We've decided what we'll do about this… business.' He settled himself into the leather armchair opposite the one that Clara had chosen as a vantage point.

'Which is?' Clara wondered whether Alistair had been able to talk any sense into Gabriel.

'I'm keen that no one here suffers any fall-out from anything that might happen to me. I was thinking of taking a step back from the charity for a while, but Alistair disagrees. Apparently he had a very fruitful discussion with one of your colleagues yesterday, and he won't accept the possibility that I may become a liability. We've decided that I'll maintain my involvement here for the time being but keep the matter under review. Do you have any thoughts on that?'

It didn't matter what Clara thought. It mattered that she could keep Gabriel safe. But something about those dark eyes of his, and the sudden vulnerability in them, made her answer.

'I think that now isn't the time for you to abandon your core priorities. If the people here want to stand by you, then you should let them. Your work here clearly means a great deal to you.'

'You thought it wouldn't? What gave you the right to question my commitment?' The sudden coolness in his eyes passed and he smiled. 'The money, maybe…'

Yes, it was the money. And Gabriel's charm, which made everything seem as if it was a game to him. Clara was beginning to learn otherwise, and she flushed in embarrassment.

'Do you know how my brother died?' he asked quietly.

'Yes, I do. You were both visiting a cave, close to your parents' summer home in Italy, and you were caught in a rock fall. That must be a very difficult thing to live with. I'm sorry.'

Gabriel nodded. 'I'd find it impossible if I didn't do something in support of the people who go into dangerous situations to help others. You must understand that. You were an ambulance paramedic.'

'Yes, I do. I've seen people who work with the emergency services get hurt in the course of their jobs.'

He nodded, the warmth in his eyes telling Clara that this was exactly what he wanted to hear. That she wouldn't just support his commitment to the work of his charity, she'd put her heart into it as well. Shame he didn't know that her heart wasn't a vessel that she relied on any more.

'Thank you.' He leaned back in his seat, smiling, and suddenly the atmosphere in the office seemed to change. Being with Gabriel was a lot like being on a roller-coaster at times. 'There's another…engagement that I should mention.'

'Yes?'

'There's a cocktail party on Saturday. Alistair thought it would be better to cancel, but I've persuaded him otherwise.' Clearly the conversation between Gabriel and his fellow director had been a matter of give and take.

'You're going to a cocktail party. The day after tomorrow?'

'I'm holding one. At my place. It's not *just* a cocktail party, we've put the guest list together very carefully.'

'People who are in a position to help the charity, you mean?'

'People who share our aims. We've asked a couple of Parliamentary advisors, chief executives from companies and charities and so on…' He grinned roguishly. 'I doubt any of them will be slipping me a roofie.'

And Gabriel wouldn't call it off. Clara was learning that putting a few toes back into the water wasn't his style. It was all or nothing with him, and he had to strip off and jump straight in. Clara tried to ignore the mental picture, because the temptation to dwell on the stripping-off part made her want to fan her face.

'I'll prepare a plan of action, then. Are there any other engagements I should know about?'

He shrugged. 'I'm going to Italy for a few days in a couple of weeks' time. It's the anniversary of my brother's death and I always go back, to be with my parents. In between then and now…

I guess that anything that happens will be just as much of a surprise to me as it is to you.'

'Okay. I'm sure we can handle it.'

'Great.' He got to his feet. 'Now that's settled, I need to go and see the Dream Team.'

'Who?' Clara picked up her bag, ready to follow him.

'Come and meet them.' He shot the words over his shoulder. 'I think you might like them.'

The Dream Team was located on the next floor up, in a large office that contained three desks, some seriously hi-tech computer equipment and a lot of clutter. The muted colours of the offices below were replaced with posters and whiteboards, with a couple of bright purple sofas in one corner. An inflatable gorilla sat at one of the desks and the other two were occupied by a pair who seemed barely out of their teens. The young woman was concentrating on a large screen in front of her, and her companion was fiddling with his phone.

'This is Kaia and Alfie.' Gabriel frowned at the gorilla. 'Where's Ben?'

Alfie pulled a face and Kaia looked up apologetically from her screen. 'He's…gone home to get some sleep.'

'And how long was he up for this time?'

Alfie and Kaia exchanged glances, and Gabriel rolled his eyes. 'Okay, I don't really need to know the details. Tell him that I won't have any more all-nighters from him.'

Kaia shrugged. 'He gets involved with what he's doing, and he loses track of time. You know Ben…'

'Yes, I do. And I know that he gets results, but I won't have him doing it at the expense of his own health. If he can't get into some kind of a routine where he eats and sleeps regularly, I'm going to have to…' Gabriel shrugged. 'I'll think of something. Just tell him.'

'Will do, boss.' Alfie grinned.

'While you're at it, you might mention that if he tries coming into the office at the weekend, he'll find a security guard who'll politely but firmly refuse to let him in. You can organise that, Clara?'

'Yes, I can revoke his access out of working hours. And we can tactfully make sure he leaves at a reasonable hour in the evening.'

'Good. Thank you.' Gabriel turned to Kaia. 'Are you dropping by his place tonight?'

'I thought I might.'

'In that case…' Gabriel took his wallet out, extracting a couple of notes. 'Will you leave a bit early and go and get some shopping for him? Let's see if we can introduce him to fruit, shall we? And perhaps a few things he can't eat straight out of the packet?'

Kaia nodded, taking the notes and putting them in the pocket of her ripped jeans. 'Will do. Thanks.'

Gabriel nodded, and both Kaia's and Alfie's gazes turned to Clara in silent curiosity. Then Kaia stepped forward, obviously the spokesperson for the two.

'Hi, I'm Kaia.'

'Clara. Alistair told you who I am?'

Kaia nodded. 'He said we mustn't get in your way.'

Gabriel chuckled. 'He means you mustn't get in *my* way. If you do then there's always the chance that one of Clara's team will spring from the shadows and tackle you to the ground.'

'Really?' Kaia's eyebrows shot up and she backed away.

'No one's getting tackled to the ground.' Clara shot Gabriel a glance, hoping it might imply it was perfectly possible that she might tackle him to the ground if he didn't stop messing around. 'My job is to make sure things never get that far.'

'Of course. Forgive me. Kaia, Alfie and Ben are our design and ideas team. Ben's alter ego is the only dangerous thing around here and all you really need to deal with him is a pin…' Gabriel gestured towards the inflatable gorilla.

'I'll bear that in mind.' Clara turned to Kaia, smiling. 'So your work is with rescue teams?'

'Partly, but not exclusively. If we have a good idea about pretty much anything, Gabriel lets us run with it.'

'Sometimes they come up with nothing. But sometimes they hit gold.' Gabriel grinned.

It all sounded a bit haphazard. This must be one of the high-risk projects that Gabriel had referred to. But if the Dream Team was as good as he obviously thought they were, then giving them free range opened up the possibility of new ideas and outside-the-box thinking. Sometimes unconventional and head in the clouds was exactly what it took to come up with undreamed-of results.

'You might find the project that Kaia and Ben are working on interesting, they're looking into 3D printing to make prosthetic limbs.'

'I've read a little about that, it's got some great applications. This is one of the projects that falls slightly outside your core interests?'

'It has all sorts of applications…' Gabriel shrugged. 'It's not a new idea, but it's something that Alistair and I were both passionate about and Kaia and Ben felt they had something unique to add to what's already out there.'

Clara was having difficulty working out whether the team's activities were an exercise in chaos or an inspired leap of faith. When she looked into Gabriel's face, she saw only the leap of faith.

'Kaia will be happy to show you…'

He turned to Kaia and she nodded. Clara hesitated. Much as she wanted to see what Kaia was doing, her responsibility was to keep her eye on Gabriel. 'You're staying here?'

'Yes, Alfie and I have a few things we need to talk about.'

If she was going to give in, she may as well do it gracefully. 'Okay. I'd love to see what you're doing, Kaia.'

CHAPTER FIVE

GABRIEL DIDN'T WANT to think about his reasons. Wanting Clara's genuine interest, her real opinions, instead of just a reiteration of her company's policies, wasn't logical, but he wanted it anyway. And as she looked at Kaia's designs, it seemed that her defences were dropping. The brittle smile that she used on him so frequently was replaced by a softness that he was fast beginning to crave.

He was the watcher now, instead of the watched. It actually felt good that no one seemed to be taking much notice of him. Gabriel jumped as Alfie spoke.

'I can't find a way to make this work any better…' He was rolling his finger thoughtfully over the trackpad in front of him, turning the wireframe image on the screen.

'Perhaps that's the answer you're looking for, then. There's no guaranteed answer to any of the problems we set you.'

'Yeah.' Alfie couldn't take his eyes from the screen. Something was still bugging him.

And in a world where everything he'd thought was concrete seemed to be crumbling, and the only thing that Gabriel was completely sure of were his beliefs, there was only one question to ask.

'Do you *believe* you can come up with something better?'

'Yeah, I do. I haven't made any solid progress, though, and I can't see a good reason to spend any more time and money on it.'

And yet… Gabriel could tell that Alfie wasn't satisfied.

'I'll worry about the cost. If you believe in it, that's reason enough to run with it for a little longer. Touch base with me at the end of next week, and let me know how you're doing.'

'Yeah, okay. Thanks…' Alfie's attention wandered back to the wireframe rendering on the screen, and Gabriel's gaze was drawn to Clara.

Kaia had just put one of the prototype prosthetic limbs into her hands and she was turning it over, inspecting it carefully. The look on Clara's face told him that she knew exactly how much this would mean to a child. To hundreds of children, if the dream could be translated into a reality.

He wondered what had made Clara give up medicine. She was very good at her job but it didn't seem to hold much passion for her. He knew that a paramedic's life could be hard, and was often taxing, but Clara didn't seem to be afraid of hard or taxing. Being a doctor was one of the things that gave Gabriel hope and a reason to be alive, and yet Clara had turned her back on her medical career. Despite himself, he very much wanted to know why.

The package from her head office had been delivered straight into Clara's hands, as was customary with anything important. She'd had a brief chance to look at the contents while Gabriel and Alistair were talking over lunch, and the news wasn't good. Clara's stomach tightened into knots at the thought of having to deliver this blow.

She waited until the team had accompanied them home. After the noise and heat of the London streets in the early afternoon, his house seemed cool and calm. Gabriel ushered her into the sitting room, closing the door behind them.

'Are you going to tell me what's wrong?'

Clara had thought she'd made a pretty good job of covering her dismay. Gabriel took off his jacket, throwing himself down in one of the easy chairs and motioning her towards another.

'Come on. It can't be *that* bad.'

Not in comparison to the life-threatening events his charity dealt with. Or in the context of Gabriel's unfailing optimism. Clara reminded herself that she was being unprofessional and that she was there to support him, not the other way around.

'I have your new phone.' She took the padded envelope from her bag, sliding the handset across the table towards him. 'Not as smart as your other one, I'm afraid, but it's a good deal more secure. All your contacts and other information have been transferred over and it's fully charged and ready for use.'

He picked up the phone, turning it thoughtfully in his hands. 'It's got…a certain utilitarian chic. What was the matter with the other one?'

Clara took a breath. 'We found software that was capable of tracking your location along with your texts and conversations. It also has the capability of turning the microphone on when the phone's not in use, making the phone into a listening device.'

He stared at her. 'So—you're telling me I've been bugged? Someone's been tracking my movements and listening to everything I say.'

'Yes.'

She could see it in his eyes. The realisation that his privacy had been violated and there was nothing he could do about it.

'I suppose it's a normal reaction to be trying to remember every conversation I've had in the last two months, since I got that phone…' Gabriel wiped his hands across his face, shaking his head.

'I suppose so.' Clara couldn't think of anything more reassuring to say.

'I'll just have to make the effort not to do it, then.' His smile would convince anyone that nothing was wrong, and Clara wondered how many times it had fooled her into thinking that Gabriel didn't understand the seriousness of the situation. 'Is there anything else?'

'Yes, we've found out where the flunitrazepam came from. There was an empty water bottle in your recycling bin that contained traces of the drug. It's not your usual brand, so maybe you remember it?'

Clara slid the photograph of the bottle out of the envelope, and he took it from her, staring at it.

'Do you remember where you got the water from? It would have been just before you went to dinner.' She prompted him gently.

'Not really… Wait a minute, yes, I do. Someone gave it to me.' He tossed the photograph onto the table as if it had just burned his fingers, and sprang to his feet. Staring out through the front windows at the quiet street seemed to calm him a little. Or maybe he just didn't want her to see his face. Clara was learning that the most private part of Gabriel's life was his pain.

'I go running most days after work, and usually take a couple of turns around the park. I know most of the regulars…'

He sighed, and Clara waited, studying his back. Even Gabriel needed a little time to get his head around this.

'It was a warm evening, and I'd slowed down to drink some water. A woman ran into me from behind, and knocked the bottle out of my hand…

She and her friend were all apologies, and they insisted I take one of theirs.' He shook his head. 'They were really nice.'

The people who hurt you the most usually *were* really nice. You had to get close to someone to really hurt them.

'It was that easy?' He was still staring through the window.

'No, it's not easy at all. They would have had to know your routine, and give you the water without arousing suspicion. I know it doesn't seem this way, but this is a step forward. We know what we're up against now.'

He shrugged. 'I never thought… How do you deal with it? Knowing all the ways that someone can invade your life, how do you ever bring yourself to trust anyone?'

There was a simple answer to that, but it wasn't the one that Gabriel needed to hear. Clara *didn't* trust anyone, and it wasn't as a result of her job.

'*Do* you trust anyone?' Gabriel had turned suddenly and his gaze was searching her face.

'I trust my team, and I trust what I know. I know that this isn't the way you'll have to live from now on, and that we can help you take your life back.'

'Nice.' He smiled suddenly. 'When in doubt always resort to the professional answer.'

'I find it's a great deal less taxing on the imagination than charming insouciance.' She couldn't resist teasing him back and Gabriel laughed.

'You think I'm insouciant?' Before Clara could think of a suitable retort he held his hand up. 'Don't answer that, I've a feeling I won't like it. Does my father know about these test results?'

'Not yet. I wanted to tell you first. I can call him if you'd like.'

'I'd be grateful if you would. I'll call him this evening.' Gabriel picked the new phone up from the coffee table. 'You're sure that no one's listening in on this one? I'd hate for anyone else to have to put up with his endlessly boring observations about my personal safety.'

'No one's listening. But I'm afraid I have some more boring observations and questions myself…'

'I'm sure yours will be delightful. Shall we do them over a glass of wine?' He got to his feet.

'Not for me, thanks.'

'Working. Of course. I can't drink alone, though, so maybe you'll indulge me by letting me make you tea. You decide whether or not you want to drink it.' Gabriel shot her a smile and swept from the room.

Gabriel might change his mind when he heard what she had to say. The list that the investigation team had prepared was pretty standard, but she had a feeling that Gabriel wouldn't relish the questions any more than she wanted to hear the answers.

He returned, holding a glass of red wine and a cup of tea, which he set down on the coffee table.

'So… I'm wondering from the look on your face exactly how much I'm not going to like this talk of ours.'

'It's just routine.' Clara was beginning to wish that Gabriel's mood radar was a bit less accurate. 'The questions are intrusive, but it's all information we need to know. Your answers will be treated with the strictest confidentiality, and only shared with our investigation team.'

'All right, let's hear them. I can take it.' He sat down taking a sip of his wine as if to prepare himself, and Clara felt a shiver run up her spine. Each nerve ending sparking in response to the dark gaze that seemed to devour her every time he turned it onto her.

Clara cleared her throat. She couldn't skirt around this, and the only way forward was through it, so she'd better get on with it.

'Romantic involvements?' She almost fell at the first hurdle.

Gabriel nodded. 'Yes.'

'Yes?'

'I mean, yes, I have romantic involvements.'

'Can you tell me how many? In the last three years?'

'Not offhand.'

That meant that the figure was more than either he or Clara were disposed to count. 'Right. And did any of those end badly?'

He thought for a moment, and then shook his head. 'Not unless I'm very much mistaken. Isn't ending well the whole point of the exercise?'

For him, maybe. Clara couldn't pretend to the lofty heights of *many* romantic involvements, and the one she could lay claim to had ended catastrophically.

'All right. Is there any possibility that a liaison may not have ended as well as you thought? A pregnancy maybe, or someone who was very upset over a break-up? A jealous partner, or someone who felt they'd made a mistake?'

'Let's not mince words. I don't sleep with women who are married or have partners. And I'm not in the habit of persuading anyone to do anything against their wishes or their own best interests.'

Clara felt her throat dry suddenly, as she saw a small pulse beat at the side of Gabriel's brow. This clearly wasn't as easy for him as he wanted to pretend.

'I'm sorry—'

'It's all right. I know you have to ask. And the answer is that my lovers are friends. I'd know if there was a pregnancy or any bad feeling as a result of our affair.'

'Okay. Thank you. I imagine you're not going to give me any names.' Names would make the investigation team's job easier, but Clara couldn't help feeling it would be a disappointment if Gabriel did give them.

'You imagine quite correctly.' He smiled suddenly, as if trying to distance himself from all of it. 'Unless I've underestimated you, you have a list of contacts from my phone, but that's not going to do you much good because I don't sleep with everyone I talk to. And I dare say you could try to coerce the names out of me, but I'll resist for as long as I'm able…'

That might be interesting... Clara swallowed down the thought. 'In that case, I'd like you to think about whether anyone else might hold a grudge against you. If you do give me a name, I'll treat it with the greatest discretion. It would be a way of protecting that person.'

He narrowed his eyes. 'How do you justify that statement?'

The tension in the room built. Clara couldn't help glancing up at the modern glass chandelier above their heads, wondering if it was about to start reverberating in response.

'Because whoever's orchestrating this threat against you might use that grudge in a way that could be detrimental to both you and the other person involved.'

'Point taken.' Gabriel relaxed a little. 'But there's still no one.'

'Very well. In that case, the next question is about any conflicts with your colleagues at the charity or other organisations you work with…'

The questions had been exhaustive and probing, and Gabriel had struggled to keep his temper at times. His friends, his lovers, anyone and everything that meant anything to him had been carefully scrutinised. Clara had done it with as much sensitivity as possible but he felt violated.

But today had made one thing very clear to him. He couldn't avoid the violation, but he had a choice about who was going to do it. He'd rather it was Clara.

'I've come to a decision. I think we should revisit your suggestion about CCTV.'

Maybe his reluctance sounded in his voice, because Clara had the grace to hesitate. 'This is…what *you* want?'

'If I'm going to invite guests to my home on Saturday, then it would be wrong not to tell them the situation and take every measure to ensure their safety. And…when I spoke to my mother last night, she asked me to follow your recommendations.'

His mother had begged him. And while there was still room for doubt about exactly what had happened to him, Gabriel had been able to content himself with the idea that what his mother didn't know couldn't hurt her. But now he'd realised that Clara was the only thing standing between his mother and her fears for him.

'Okay. We'll find a way to install the cameras, without driving you crazy.' Clara shot him a smile and suddenly everything seemed do-able.

'I want somewhere I can be alone.' The thought came out of nowhere, and the more Gabriel clung to it, the more he liked it. 'Somewhere no one's watching or listening.'

'Would you like to pick your spot?'

A safe place. A private place. Clara seemed to understand.

'My study…and bedroom.'

'Let's make that happen, then.'

CHAPTER SIX

YESTERDAY HAD BEEN a difficult day, but it had been productive. Clara had been confident about going home for the night after Gabriel had insisted that she needed a break, and promised that he would follow the advice of the night guards. She arrived at Gabriel's house the next morning, feeling ready to take on whatever he threw at her. It turned out to be a devastating smile, and breakfast.

'You haven't eaten?' He relieved her of her jacket and laptop bag, then took the takeaway cup from her hand, flipping open the lid and wrinkling his nose.

'Hey! That's my coffee!' Clara plumped herself down at the kitchen table as he tipped the contents of the cup into the sink.

'It's lukewarm. And I doubt it tasted much like coffee, even when it was hot.'

He had a point. The smell of fresh ground coffee as he tamped the filter holder and inserted it into the machine was much more tempting. He set a cup and saucer in front of her, together with a small jug of frothed milk.

Clara took a sip. The coffee had enough bite for the morning but was still mellow and smooth. 'This is nice. Thank you.'

He nodded. 'You like strawberries?'

'Doesn't everybody? What's all this, Gabriel?'

'This is our revenge. For yesterday.' He turned the heat on under a crêpe pan that stood ready on the cooker and took a jug of batter from the fridge.

His energy was seductive. The way he moved… Clara didn't want to think about the way he moved. Dressed in a pair of jeans and a casual shirt, he was just what any woman would want to wake up to. Add the coffee and the cooking and he was downright irresistible. Clara sank her head into her hands.

'And living well is the best revenge?'

He poured a measure of batter into the pan and turned, shooting her a melting smile. It was the kind of smile that could get her into a lot of trouble, and was far more challenging than anything she'd faced with Gabriel so far.

'Don't you think so?'

Clara's definition of living well had been to retreat from the battlefield that her parents had turned their family into. To defy Tim's betrayal by making a life for herself that didn't allow for the possibility of being hurt again. It involved getting a job and a home that no one could take from her, and coffee and crêpes with the most gorgeous man she'd ever seen hadn't seemed a logical first step.

Maybe they should have been. Gabriel's way of appreciating the good things in life and his refusal to court despair for very long were all part of his charm, and this was very clearly an act of defiance, aimed at the unknown people who wanted to do him harm.

'I can give it a whirl. Breakfast first, and then I'll show you the schematics for the cameras.'

He chuckled. 'You see what a great team we make? You have a wealth of practical suggestions, and I have coffee and crêpes…'

Maybe it was the lure of the unobtainable. Gabriel pondered the question as he followed Clara around the house, nodding his acceptance of all the camera placements. In any other circumstances, with any other woman, he would have made the first steps towards seduction already, taking careful heed of the signs that told him whether his attentions were welcome or not. But seduction seemed far too commonplace for someone like Clara, and in any case she was far too professional to allow herself to be caught up in a whirlwind affair with someone she was working with. It was one of the things he respected about her.

'You're not really that interested, are you?' Clara's voice intruded suddenly on his thoughts.

'What? Sorry, I was distracted for a moment. What did you say?'

'I said we'd be making regular sweeps for bugs. Is that all right?'

'Yes, of course.' Yesterday's discovery that someone had been listening in on him still made his spine crawl. 'I appreciate that. Shouldn't I have some kind of device that I can carry around? That warns me if there's anything in the vicinity?'

Clara gave him a searching look. 'I could give you a pocket scanner. But I'm not going to.'

'Why?' Gabriel suspected that he'd let his paranoia slip. 'Are you handling me again?'

Clara didn't bat an eyelash. 'Yes, I am. I dare

say you do the same for your patients, you tell them what's happening, but they really don't need to know the details. Just that you're doing your job and they're safe.'

Touché. Gabriel hadn't had much sleep last night, and had got out of bed more than once to inspect all the electrical equipment in the room for signs of tampering. He'd made an effort to start the day on a more positive note, but even the pleasure of having breakfast with Clara hadn't changed his mood for long.

'Are you going to your office today? I can call the CCTV installation team and get them to set up the cameras while you're out.'

She was gently pushing him back to work. Clara knew that it was the only thing that made any sense to him at the moment and the thought of kicking his heels here, thinking about CCTV cameras, and how his home was no longer a safe place, didn't much appeal to Gabriel.

'You're right. Alistair's out of the office today and we have a team of volunteers coming in. I should be there to thank them personally. Will you be ready to go in half an hour?'

That seemed to be the answer that Clara was looking for. 'We're ready whenever you are.'

* * *

Gabriel had appeared thoughtful in the car, but as soon as he got to The Watchlight Trust's offices, he seemed to pull himself out of his reverie. It was just as Clara had hoped.

He made straight for the conference room, making sure that the dozen men and women around the conference table, who were addressing and stuffing envelopes, had coffee, tea and whatever other refreshments they wanted. He thanked everyone, stopping to talk and answer questions, and then marched across to the Dream Team's office. Ben was there today, a slender young man with tousled hair and glasses, and as Clara found a seat for herself in the corner she saw Gabriel quietly impressing the need for a more regular routine on him.

This suited him. His concern for other people seemed to chase away his preoccupation with his own situation. Clara had seen plenty of people crumble under the kind of pressure that Gabriel was experiencing, and yet he was finding a way to deal with it.

A muffled bump from outside the room, and the sound of voices, jerked her to her feet. Gabriel was already heading towards the door to see what was happening, and Clara took hold of his arm, pulling him back.

'Ladies first…' He murmured the words quietly, and his sudden smile seemed just for her. Clara shot him an exasperated look.

'No, Security first.' She opened the door, looking outside, and saw a grey-haired man hurrying across from the conference room.

'Is Gabriel there? Emma's hurt herself…'

'Doctors first, in this case…' Gabriel threw the words over his shoulder as he strode past her, following the man back to the conference room.

Clara could hear the sound of crying, and the knot of people parted as they saw Gabriel. A young woman was seated on one of the chairs, cradling one hand against her chest. Gabriel knelt down in front of her.

'Okay, Emma. Let me see.'

Emma shook her head, rocking back and forth. Shock, perhaps. Gabriel turned to the man who had come to fetch him.

'What happened, John?'

'She tripped over and put her arm out to break her fall. She's hurt herself, but she won't let anyone touch her.'

'Thanks. Perhaps we should give her a bit of space.'

John nodded, shepherding the rest of the volunteers out of the room, while Gabriel turned back to Emma. He pulled up a chair, sitting down and leaning towards her.

'Emma. Emma, look at me.'

Emma twisted away from him, still cradling her right arm protectively. It was then that Clara saw the reason for her reaction. Three of the fingers from her left hand were missing, leaving only the thumb and forefinger.

Clara knew from her work as a paramedic that people who had injuries to one hand were very protective of the other, and tended to panic if they hurt it. Gabriel had to deal with Emma's instinctive reaction before he could give her any medical attention.

'Okay.' Gabriel laid one hand lightly on Emma's back. 'Just give me a status report, then, eh?'

'Might be a Colles' fracture…' Emma clearly had some medical knowledge. And Gabriel was using that to help her to distance herself from her situation.

'I'll bet that hurts.' Gabriel's voice was gentle.

Emma nodded, tears running down her face. 'How could I be so stupid?'

'You're not stupid. You had an accident, that's all, and you know we can fix this.' Gabriel put his arm carefully around Emma's shoulder and suddenly she leaned into his chest, sobbing.

It was hard to focus on what she was supposed to be doing. All of Clara's instincts were telling her that she should be helping care for Emma, but that wasn't her job. And Gabriel was all Emma needed right now.

She was beginning to calm down, and slowly took her arm away from her chest, allowing him to see it. The wrist was already red and swollen, and there was a slight deformity, which indicated that Emma had been right in her assessment and there was a break at the lower end of one of the two long bones in her forearm.

'I'm going to need an X-ray. We'll go over to the clinic.'

'Thanks. Sorry…' Emma was regaining her composure quickly.

'You've nothing to be sorry about. Clara, we'll use the staff entrance.' Gabriel flashed Clara a glance and she nodded. The door in the hallway that led straight through into the clinic next door had been equipped with state-of-the-art locks and alarms to make sure that anyone who did get into the charity's offices couldn't access the clinic.

Gabriel helped Emma to her feet, his arm around her to support her, and walked her out into the corridor. When she stood up, her dark hair fell back from her face, and exposed a deep scar running across the left side of her jaw and down her neck. She'd been hurt very badly at some point and from the looks of the scar it had been relatively recently.

'You're the security officer?' Emma looked at her as she activated the handprint scanner and then punched in the code for the door.

'Yes, that's right.' Gabriel answered Emma's question. 'Although Clara used to be one of yours—a paramedic.'

'Yeah?' Emma shot her a watery smile. 'Bet you wouldn't be making so much fuss.'

'I'd be crying like a baby. Don't take any nonsense from him, you know how doctors can be.'

Gabriel chuckled and Emma smiled again. Slowly she was regaining control of the situation and it was clearly making her feel much better.

A nurse saw them and hurried towards Gabriel,

and he asked her to fetch a wheelchair. She returned almost immediately and Gabriel settled Emma into the chair, wheeling her along a short stretch of corridor to the X-ray suite.

Clara couldn't imagine that the clinic didn't have an X-ray technician and nurses to help as it had a quiet air of being well run and fully staffed. But Gabriel was doing everything himself, talking to Emma all the while. Clara could see that Emma trusted him and only seemed distressed when anyone else came near her.

A few minutes later they went to a comfortable consulting room to view the X-rays, and Gabriel raised the backrest of the examination couch, holding the tablet out in front of Emma so she could see for herself.

'What do you reckon? I'd say we need to set it and then put a temporary cast on. I'll replace it when the swelling goes down…' Gabriel stated the obvious, and Emma nodded.

'What do you want? I've got analgesics and you can have a mild sedative.'

'Paracetamol will do me.' Emma turned the corners of her mouth down.

Gabriel gave a nod, and then stood up, opening the door and beckoning to the nurse outside to come and sit with Emma. Clara followed him to the dispensary.

'You *can't* just give her paracetamol…' This was out of order on so many levels. A former paramedic telling a doctor what he could and couldn't do. A security consultant meddling in the affairs of a client…

'I know.' He puffed out a breath. 'Emma was attacked on duty nine months ago by a guy with a machete. She lost a lot of blood and woke up to find that she'd lost three fingers. She's never quite forgiven the team that took her to the hospital for not managing to find them.'

'So she needs to be in control.' Clara felt a little stupid for having interfered.

'Yes. And as my own experience a few days ago demonstrates, a sedative isn't going to help much with that.' Gabriel shot Clara a knowing smile, handing her a couple of bulky packets of dressings. 'Since you're helping me, you can carry those.'

Right. She wasn't supposed to be helping him, she was meant to be protecting him. But the clinic was secure, and she may as well make herself useful.

When they returned, Gabriel sat down beside

Emma, laying out the strong analgesics he'd brought with him so that Emma could see them. 'Are you really going to make me hurt you that much, Emma? You can trust me.'

Emma's eyes filled with tears. 'I don't want this, Gabriel.'

'I know, and I don't blame you. But let's do it the right way, eh? You and I.'

Gabriel's skill as a doctor was obvious. Emma didn't flinch as he slid the needle into her arm, delivering a local anaesthetic. The setting of the broken bone in her wrist was done with the help of another doctor from the clinic and the minimum of fuss. He worked quickly, making sure that everything was done right first time, so as to cause Emma as little distress as possible. When the preliminary dressings were applied and the second X-ray was taken, she smiled.

'Nice job.'

'You too.' Gabriel grinned at her. 'You'll be good to go shortly, although you may as well stay and have some lunch. Is your husband going to join you?'

'If that's okay. Steve will be along to pick me up in a minute.' Gabriel had called Emma's husband and let her speak with him before the bone in her wrist had been set.

'Great. Lunch for two, then.' Gabriel picked up the phone and asked for a menu to be brought up.

'You'll call me?' His face became serious for a moment.

'I'm okay.' Emma gave him a smile.

'Yeah, I know. Call me anyway. This evening. Just to relieve me of the need to call you.'

'All right. I'll call.'

Gabriel had waited for Emma's husband to arrive before going back to work, and when the clinic called through to tell him that they were leaving, he'd gone back to talk to Emma again. He'd clearly been there for her after the attack, and he was there for her now, reminding her yet again that this injury was just temporary and her wrist would heal.

After an afternoon spent moving from one set of decisions to another, at an almost breathtaking pace, they returned to his house to find that the CCTV installation was complete. Clara had asked where they could set the CCTV monitor up, and Gabriel had offered the basement. The last owners had used it as a games room for their three teenagers, and it was the most comfortable basement that Clara had ever seen, clean and well lit with two large sofas, a library-style table and chairs, and a kitchenette and bathroom tucked away in the corner.

It was perfect. Space to work, and set up a centre of operations for her team, who could sit down here during their breaks. An added bonus was that she would have a bolt hole. Gabriel had loitered awkwardly in the hall, allowing her to go and survey the space on her own, and it seemed that he never came down here.

It was almost a relief to spend some time away from the electricity generated by Gabriel's presence while she organised the space for her team, but finally Clara climbed the stairs to his study to discuss the arrangements for the cocktail party the following evening.

'I was beginning to feel a little lonely up here.' His study was as light and airy as the rest of the house and Gabriel was seated in one of the deep leather armchairs, surrounded by glass-fronted bookcases that occupied one end of the room.

'It's best if we can stay out of your way.' Clara looked up from the notes that he'd given her. 'You'll be able to start getting back to normal.'

'I suppose I can always email you.'

'Or you could just shout…'

The evening sun slanted through the windows, caressing her cheek as she flipped through the typed sheets. Gabriel's notes were detailed and thorough, and Clara wondered where he'd found the time to write them.

'This all looks good.' She paused, frowning slightly. 'There aren't any surprises, are there? Fireworks at midnight, or a champagne fountain in the garden?'

'No surprises. I wouldn't waste good champagne by putting it into a fountain, and tomorrow is going to be all about entertaining company and convivial surroundings. Why gild the lily?'

'All right. I'll leave the lilies to you. I'd like you to answer one thing, though.'

'Just one? Of course.'

Clara thought for a moment. She needed to choose her words carefully. 'Don't take this the wrong way but my impression is that you're pretty used to pushing things to the limit.'

He gave her a searching look. 'You're concerned that tomorrow evening is all about showing the people who are attacking my family that I won't back down? That's exactly what I want to do, but I would never put others at risk for my own gratification. Tomorrow evening will have no surprises. I'll work with you to keep things safe.'

'Thank you, Gabriel. That's all I wanted to know.'

'May I ask you a question in return?'

'That's only fair.' Up here, away from the cameras and the night guards, it felt almost as if they were in a bubble together. Almost as if the usual boundaries didn't exist.

'If something *were* to happen… If there's ever a physical confrontation…'

'If that happens, the first choice is always to secure your safety and make a retreat. As quickly as possible.'

'What about you? Who looks after your safety, and that of the team?'

Clara met his puzzled frown with a smile. Clients were usually too concerned about their own safety to consider the members of the team.

'You don't need to worry about us, we're all trained in self-defence.'

'But…' Gabriel was clearly still turning the matter over in his head.

'But what?'

He grinned suddenly. 'Could you bring me to my knees? For instance…'

Gabriel was playing, but only he would play this way. He was assessing the new normal, pushing its boundaries and finding its limits. That was what he did, and Clara suspected it was one of the things that made him very good at his job.

'You want to find out?' Clara stood up, trying to ignore the inappropriate tingle that ran down her spine.

'Now?'

'The first lesson of self-defence is that people don't usually wait for you to change into your gym clothes before they attack you. I can do it in a dress. Or is that just an excuse?'

He got to his feet slowly. 'Go ahead, then.'

'Well, you have to grab me first.'

He raised his eyebrows. Clearly grabbing women wasn't something he did all that often, and Clara could only like that about him.

'Go on. Grab me.'

He reached out, gently closing his fingers around her wrist. That would barely have restrained a fly. *If* you left out the part about his touch. His subtle scent, and the way she wanted to find out if his skin was as smooth as it looked. Gabriel had weapons of his own, and it was always unwise to underestimate an opponent. But she could handle it.

'You're not all that good at grabbing, are you?'

He chuckled. 'I'm going to take that as a compliment.'

Gabriel clearly wasn't going to try to widen his experience, so Clara would have to improvise. She reached out, guiding his hands to her shoulders, ignoring the sweet electricity of his touch as one finger seemed to caress her bare arm.

Then she moved.

Gabriel had thought that Clara was about to demonstrate a fail-safe technique for escape. But she moved so quickly that she took him off balance, and suddenly he found himself up close and personal with her. And at her mercy.

Clara had stepped to one side, and her right hand was at the back of his left bicep, his arm twisted back at an angle that threatened pain if she went any further. He tried to pull away and she relaxed her grip a little, obviously giving him some room to move without releasing him from the hold.

'Be still… I won't hurt you.' Her voice was clear and firm, and seemed close enough to reverberate through his whole body.

Gabriel took a breath. Adrenaline was pulsing through his veins, and perhaps that was why everything suddenly seemed so clear. If he tried, he was sure that he'd be able to feel Clara's heartbeat.

'All right. Relax…' Her voice soothed him, but when he stilled she tightened the hold a little. Not enough to hurt, but Gabriel knew that if he tried to struggle it would probably feel as if she was ripping his arm off.

'Is that it?' He wanted her to go further. Right to the limit.

'You wanted to know if I could bring you to your knees…' Clara obviously wasn't anywhere near her limit just yet.

'Yes. Do it.'

'All right. You're going down. Move with me.'

Yeah. That was all he wanted to do right now. Clara could take him wherever she wanted to go.

Slowly, she tightened her grip, bending him forward and forcing him onto his knees. His pride was long gone now, and something else replaced it. He trusted her.

'Are you okay?'

Surprisingly enough, yes. This was something real, and the thoughts of the insubstantial threats that had been bugging him over the last three days retreated at last.

'Yes. Just don't make any sudden movements, will you?'

She chuckled quietly. 'Right you are. Just follow me, we're going down a bit further.'

An iron fist, in the sweetest of velvet gloves. She moved again, and Gabriel had no choice but to follow. He found himself face down on the carpet, and felt her knee behind his shoulder, keeping him down. The grip on his arm changed a little, and he felt her free hand at the back of his other arm. She must be practically on top of him.

The thought of physical violence had always disgusted Gabriel. But this was something different. It was trust and confidence. Testing each other, going to the edge together.

'What do you call this?'

'It's a version of a hammer lock. Still all right?'

'Yes. Climbing the learning curve.' Gabriel felt a trickle of sweat running down his spine. Trapped and helpless wasn't something he ever wanted to be. But Clara made it…interesting. Without the ability to see her face, he found himself listening for every inflection in her tone. It was an unlikely intimacy.

'Have you ever done this for real?'

'Only once. Not in this job—when I was a paramedic.'

'You were attacked?'

'Yes, it was a fake call, they were after the drugs we carried. The only casualty was my own partner. I ended up treating him for a broken nose.'

Suddenly her grip on him relaxed and Gabriel rolled over to see her sitting on the floor next to him, her dress spread out around her legs. If you didn't count the glistening look in her eyes, and the slight flush of her cheeks, it would be a pose that would have been perfect for a summer picnic.

He sat up, flexing his shoulder. The instinct to touch her, to make some gesture that acknowledged what had just happened between them, was impossible to resist and he reached out for her hand. When his fingers touched hers, she moved them away. But when his gaze met hers they seemed locked together still.

'Will you trust me, Clara?'

Trust didn't come easily for her. But when he reached for Clara's hand again, she didn't move. Balancing her fingers lightly on his, he guided them to his lips, brushing the most dispassionate of kisses against them.

It was another exercise in taking things as far as they could. When he let her hand go, she nodded slightly, as if Clara knew that Gabriel had drawn a line that he wouldn't cross.

'So, can anyone do this hammer lock? Could you teach me?'

'You'd probably be far more effective than I am. You're strong…' Her assessing gaze made him shiver. 'Why would you want to learn?'

'Just for my own amusement.' He could see that she didn't believe him for a second. 'We've recently commissioned a study on violence against rescue workers, and learning a bit more about self-defence might help me think about the issues more clearly.'

She smiled. 'And, of course, you have to know for yourself. You can't just take anyone else's word for it.'

'I like to be as hands on in my approach as practically possible.' Maybe he should have phrased that slightly differently. The flush on Clara's cheeks seemed to deepen a half-shade, and Gabriel felt his heart beat a little faster.

'Okay.' If her heart was beating faster too, she disguised it admirably. 'Maybe I can. Let's get tomorrow over first, shall we?'

'Yes.' Gabriel got to his feet, holding out his hand to help her up. He'd answered one question at least. However much Clara tried to hide it, she too wanted to know where the limits of their relationship lay.

CHAPTER SEVEN

CAUGHT UP IN the preparations for the cocktail party this evening, counting bottles and proclaiming that the patio lights were all wrong and needed to be done again, Gabriel seemed more relaxed than Clara had ever seen him. He was getting to grips with his situation, and if it took being forced to the floor with an armlock, then that was what it took.

Something had happened. There had been a moment when they'd both been at one with each other. The feel of his body, and hers. Knowing how his would react and understanding that he was trusting her. But Clara couldn't think about that because she had just one, overarching goal. Keep him safe.

Halfway through the afternoon, and Clara was beginning to feel a sense of satisfaction. Then her phone rang.

'Clara… He's on the move.' Instinctively Clara took a couple of steps towards the back windows.

She'd seen Gabriel sizing up the camera angles that morning, and the back of the house was the way she would have chosen to make a surreptitious exit as well.

'All right. Thanks, I'll deal with it.' She put her phone into her pocket and hurried through to the kitchen, where the caterers had taken up residence. Ducking out of their way, she glanced towards the hook that usually housed Gabriel's car keys and saw that it was empty.

She had to be quick. Grabbing her bag from the hallway, she ran down the front steps of the house into the street outside, where the small run-around that Gabriel used was parked.

He appeared just on schedule, turning out of the narrow path that led from the back of his garden onto the end of the street and sauntering along the pavement as if he had nowhere in particular to go. Maybe he didn't and this was all just a game to him. When he saw Clara, leaning against his car, his pace hardly faltered.

'Hello, there.' He gave her an urbane smile.

'Hello. Going for a walk?' Clara tried to keep the irritation from her tone.

'No, a drive.' He held up his car keys.

'And you didn't think to tell anyone? I thought we'd worked this one out, Gabriel.'

'Private business.' He moved towards the car door as if that was the end of the matter, and Clara shifted to block his path. If last night had taught her one thing, it was that Gabriel was pretty much incapable of pushing a woman out of the way.

'Here's the thing.' She folded her arms in an indication that she wasn't going to shift until she'd had her say. 'You can do whatever you want to. Go wherever you want to go. But it's a waste of money to engage security consultants and then decide that you'll play games and give us the slip.'

He nodded, giving her his most alluring smile. That wasn't going to work either. Scratch that, it worked extremely well, but it wasn't going to make her move.

'Game over. You got me. And I'm duly impressed by your vigilance. I'll be back in an hour or so…'

Maybe she needed to be a little more direct.

'Look, I know you want to push things and face the risk. But this isn't the time or the place to confront whatever demons are driving you…'

Something in his eyes told her that she'd hit home. Gabriel shook his head slightly, as if to dispel the blow.

'You're right.' He leaned forward, putting one hand on the roof of the car beside her arm. Almost touching her but not quite. 'But on this occasion, and despite your remarkable skills, you've come to the wrong conclusion. I need to go somewhere and it's a matter of urgency. So I'd be grateful if you'd forget all about whatever method of physical restraint you're considering and move aside. I'll be back in an hour.'

This wasn't just one of Gabriel's games, he was serious. Clara took a breath. Maybe this visit he was so fired up about was to a woman friend, in which case her presence would probably not be welcomed.

'We know how to be discreet, Gabriel. If this is someone with whom you have a personal relationship…'

He gave her a piercing look. 'The last time I sneaked out of the house to meet a woman I was eighteen years old. I'm going to see a patient.'

'Do you have to go yourself? Isn't there someone else available?'

'No. Mike's a friend, he's an army bomb disposal expert who's helped us out a lot with his expertise. He was injured himself a year ago.'

This was a debt of friendship. There was no way that Clara was going to be able to talk Gabriel out of going.

'Then we'll take you and sit outside in the car.'

Gabriel shook his head. 'Mike has PTSD. Two guys parked outside in an SUV is definitely *not* going to work for him. He can be a little paranoid at times.'

'All right. I know that people with PTSD can be challenged by the unexpected, and I know how to respond to that. Let me at least drive you.'

'You'll have to come inside with me.'

'Okay, then, so I'll come inside. You can trust me, Gabriel.'

He thought for a moment and then nodded. 'All right.'

Clara was tight-lipped as she drove. Gabriel didn't blame her. They could very easily have had that conversation in the house and probably come to the same conclusion. He should give her a little more credit, and realise that the Clara who did her job so efficiently wasn't so very different from the one he'd seen last night. The one he liked, and trusted.

He called Mike from the car, giving him the registration number of the SUV that Clara was driving and telling him that he wasn't coming alone. When they drew up outside the house, he ventured some information.

'Maybe we play down the protection aspect of things.'

'Yes. Okay.' Clara was clearly still annoyed with him and Gabriel wondered whether he'd made a mistake. Her brisk, no-nonsense manner wasn't what Mike needed at the moment. He needed the Clara Gabriel had woken up to three mornings ago.

'Don't lie to him. But don't worry him either.'

'I know how to handle this, Gabriel.' Suddenly her voice was softer and Gabriel realised that there was no danger of Mike not getting the Clara who understood. She was just withholding that from him at the moment.

She followed him up the front path, standing back as Gabriel rang the bell. He heard the sound of Mike's crutches in the hallway, then silence as he checked who was there before he shot the bolts back.

When he opened the door, Mike gave him a relaxed grin, which Gabriel knew was entirely manufactured. He went with the flow.

'Hi, Mike. This is Clara, she's working with me at the moment.'

'Hello. Pleased to meet you.' Clara's voice was quiet and would have reassured the angriest of hearts, the way it had been when he'd opened his eyes and first seen her. He'd wondered whether that had been a figment of his imagination.

Mike hesitated, looking her over, and she smiled. Then he beckoned them inside, closing and locking the front door behind them. Gabriel wondered whether Clara had noticed the piece of paper pinned to the doorframe, listing the registration numbers of all the cars parked in the street.

Mike ushered them into the spotless sitting room, and Clara turned to him. 'I'll make myself scarce while you and Gabriel talk. Would you like me to make some tea?'

'You came to make tea?' Mike shot her an amused look. 'Sit down and tell me a bit about yourself.'

'Okay. Thanks.' Clara sat down on one end of the sofa and Mike lowered himself into a chair opposite her. The empty leg of his jeans was pinned up this morning, and he obviously hadn't got around to putting on his prosthetic.

'Let me guess.' Mike had played this game with most of the charity's staff, and Gabriel had hoped he might give it a miss with Clara. 'Social worker?'

'Not even close.' Clara smiled at him. 'I started off as a paramedic with the London Ambulance Service and then spent two years as an Army Reserve medic. I'm working with Gabriel on a personal safety project.'

It was a good answer. Entirely truthful, and yet giving no cause for alarm. Gabriel wondered if Clara had put the same thought into the answers she'd given him at the hospital, and supposed she probably had.

Mike nodded. 'Two years. You must have re-enlisted, then?'

'Yes, I did. When I got back home after my first tour, things were…different.' Gabriel thought he saw a flash of vulnerability on Clara's face.

'Yeah. Things are different all right. I served in an EOD unit.'

'Then I probably owe you one. The EOD units in our area saved a lot of lives.'

'I just did my job. Left my leg behind, though. Your lot made sure that it was below the knee and not above, so I guess I owe you one too.'

The respect between them was almost tangible. Perhaps Gabriel should be the one to go and make the tea, but he wanted to stay and listen.

'So how were things different? When you came home?' Mike had relaxed now.

'Lots of ways. I found that I didn't have my marriage any more.'

Gabriel swallowed hard. It shouldn't come as any shock that Clara had been married. It was a little harder to understand how anyone could let her go.

'Yeah? I managed to dodge that bullet, I never did get married.'

Clara grinned. 'Well, there's still time. Maybe you should try standing still.'

'Oh, I'm good at that.' Mike snorted with laughter. 'Some days I don't go out of the house. Triggers, you know…'

'What are your triggers?'

'Rain. I remember lying in the mud, watching a puddle fill up and listening for the chopper that was coming to evacuate me. The police had helicopters up last night and I didn't get much sleep.'

Mike had described the night horrors to Gabriel already. He'd left out a few important details in this account, but it had been months before they'd got to that place of trust.

'You need a break?' Gabriel had told Mike that he could call him any time that things got too much, and he suspected that this was the purpose of his visit today.

'I don't want to go back to the clinic. I think I need to…move on. That course you told me about, I don't suppose you could swing me a place?'

'That's not going to be a problem. I'll make a few calls and see what's available.' A place in the near future was going to take quite a bit of swinging, but it was probably better that Mike didn't know about that. 'I'll make some tea…'

Mike chuckled softly. 'So it's the doctors who make the tea now, then?'

Clara sat back in her seat, crossing her legs. 'Seems so. Between you and me, I'm rather looking forward to that.'

He'd heard them talking from the kitchen. Clara's voice was quiet and relaxed, and Mike was obviously beginning to leave the terrors of last night behind. When he delivered two mugs of tea to them, they were laughing over something, and Gabriel retreated back into the kitchen to make his calls. He hadn't anticipated that Clara would be such an asset, and he'd wondered whether she might be persuaded to come and chat with a few more of his patients.

'How does next week suit you, Mike?' He'd had to call in a few favours, but he'd got the place that he wanted.

'Next week would be great. I didn't expect anything so soon, are you sure that's okay?'

'Yeah, no problem. They had a cancellation and they were pleased to fill the place. I've given Isabelle a call and she'll drop in this evening and see how you're going.' Isabelle was the clinic's outreach worker and she and Mike already had a good relationship.

'Thanks a lot. I really appreciate it.' Mike stood, leaning on his crutches as he shook Gabriel's hand and Clara disappeared into the kitchen with the empty cups. 'You didn't say you had a security team following you around.'

'It's a minor problem. Nothing really to do with me, it's my father's company that's in a bit of a bind.' Gabriel frowned. 'Clara told you?'

'No, a little bird did.' Gabriel raised his eyebrows and Mike chuckled. 'I was talking about how difficult it was to get another job, and I mentioned that I'd been thinking about security work...'

A car roared past in the street outside, and Mike jumped, twisting round. When he turned back to Gabriel his hand was shaking.

'I know. It's not the best idea I've ever had.' Mike said it before Gabriel could. 'Not much use for a security guard who can't deal with sudden noises.'

'Look at what you've done already, you have the guts to do whatever you set your mind to. Maybe the security thing could wait for a while, though.' Gabriel reinforced the theme that had run through much of Mike's counselling in the last months.

Mike nodded. 'Well, Clara asked about my qualifications and she said I was setting my sights too low, and that if I was interested in security work then going for something like consultancy might suit me better.'

'That sounds a bit more like it. If it's what you want to do, I can make some enquiries...'

'Thanks. Clara's given me her number and

said I could call her whenever I was ready. She's got contacts who can show me the ropes, and if things work out she'll try and swing me an interview. I reckon she's not working with you as a paramedic, is she?'

Gabriel chuckled. 'No, she isn't. And that's a good offer. The company she works for is the best in the business. She gave you her number?' He realised that he didn't have Clara's number.

'You haven't got her number yet? You must be slipping, mate.'

'Suppose I must be. I've had things on my mind.' Clara, mostly.

Mike nodded. 'You'd tell me if there was a reason to worry about this?'

Maybe Gabriel would, and maybe he wouldn't. Mike had worrying down to an art. But, then, despite the paranoia and the sleepless nights, his bravery and common sense had still stayed intact. He was the same person, just living under intolerable pressure.

'I leave the worrying to Clara.'

'I imagine she's the kind who has things under control.' Mike's grin implied that he included Gabriel in that.

'Yes, she does. And what about you? You'd tell me if there was any reason to worry?'

'Yeah. I just got to the point where if I didn't have something more to aim for I'd go crazy. Now I've got two things.' Mike jerked his thumb at the notepad that contained Clara's number.

'And you'll call me if that changes.'

'Yes. Thanks, I'll call.'

Clara had been silent again during their drive home, but not so tight-lipped. Gabriel supposed that she was just concentrating and it occurred to him that she was doing the work of two. Normally a driver wasn't expected to also cover protection.

'So what's this course that Mike's going on?' With the departure of the caterers the bustle in the house had subsided considerably, and when they walked through to the kitchen together, they found it deserted.

'It's a place in Hertfordshire. They run crisis courses, but also do various different follow-up courses for people with PTSD, which a lot of our patients have found valuable. Mike told me you left your number with him.'

'I hope that was all right.'

'It's fine. He's talked about security work before, but I think consultancy is a much better use of his skill-set. He's lost a lot of confidence.'

Clara nodded. 'He seems like the kind of guy who deserves all the help he can get. He's held the line, and paid a high price for it.'

Clara had held the line too, and from what she'd said to Mike she'd also paid a price. Last night, up in his study, Gabriel would have asked about that price but now it seemed impossible. She'd come out from behind her barrier of professionalism for Mike, but that had been out of respect and in response to a need. Gabriel wondered what her motive had been last night. Respect or need?

He watched as she drifted over to the counter top, lifting the edge of the foil that covered one of the platters that the caterers had left.

'They look nice.' She'd managed to peel the foil back without tearing it.

'They are. I tried them earlier on. Have one.'

She was tempted. And she resisted the temptation. 'It's all arranged so beautifully. I don't want to spoil the pattern.' Clara closed the foil again, squeezing the edges to secure them.

'Maybe you'll be off duty long enough to try

one at the party.' Suddenly it seemed important that she would be. That Clara might take just a couple of minutes off to enjoy the evening.

'I'll be needing my wits about me, then. Just in case you decide to slip away under the cover of the night.' Her smile told him that she was only half joking.

'Yeah... Look, I'm sorry about this afternoon, Clara. I didn't think.'

She turned to him, eyeing him coolly. 'You didn't think? I reckon that thinking is exactly what you *did* do.'

Gotcha. He was caught in the web of her gaze, and it was impossible to make anything more than a half-hearted effort to free himself. 'Maybe...'

He tried to turn away and she caught his arm. 'There's no maybe about it. You made a calculated decision to go alone, because you thought it would be the best thing for Mike. You put him first, even though it meant taking a risk, but you'd prefer to charm everyone into believing that you're just reckless.'

'And my charm doesn't work on you.' Gabriel turned the corners of his mouth down in an expression of mock chagrin. Somehow it felt hollow in the face of Clara's honesty.

'I imagine your charm works on me…in much the way it should.'

Nicely avoided. 'I'll take that thought up to my study with me. I've a few calls to make before I get ready for this evening.'

CHAPTER EIGHT

ONE THING THAT you could say about Gabriel was that he knew how to give a party a lot of class. His guests couldn't arrive too early or too late for him, and he greeted each one of them as if they'd come at exactly the right time. Everything was going smoothly, oiled by Gabriel's ability to make everyone that he spoke to feel that they were the only person in the room.

Clara watched as he welcomed a Parliamentary advisor, complimenting her on her dress and effortlessly disengaging her from her husband's arm. She was introduced to Alistair and Clara heard him answering her questions about the charity's newest initiatives while Gabriel kept her husband busy. The teamwork was seamless, and equal to anything her own team could accomplish.

It was easy to watch him. Less easy to tear her gaze away from him. It took practice to put the right people together, and to make it all seem so effortless.

Finally, Gabriel saw the last of his guests off and they were the only people in the room.

'Would you like a drink now?' He walked into the kitchen, where rows of bottles containing every kind of spirit and flavouring had been lined up on the counter. 'Seems a shame to let fresh peach purée go to waste. Although maybe Bellinis aren't your style.'

'I shouldn't really have a drink at all.'

'You've been on duty for sixteen hours now. Clock off and give the night guards their turn.' His smile was enticing.

'Okay. What *is* my style, then?' Clara sat down on one of the high stools next to the counter.

'I think…' His brow furrowed in thought. 'Nothing too sweet and no bubbles, but not bitters either.' He selected bottles from the range in front of him, pouring the ingredients into the cocktail shaker without measuring them. Clara raised her eyebrows.

'I think it's better to measure by instinct. Each occasion is different.'

'Of course. Silly me for expecting anything else.'

He grinned at her, giving the cocktail a good shake before pouring it. With a final flourish he added a twist of lemon peel to the rim of the glass.

'An Aviation.' The delicate violet colour from the *crème de violette* was unmistakeable. 'You're going old-school, then.'

'I prefer to think of it as a classic.' Gabriel set the glass down in front of her, watching Clara intently as she took a sip.

'Mmm. Perfect, thank you. That's a very good choice. Shame you'll never be able to re-create this.'

'Don't you think that adds something?'

Somehow it did. She'd never have this moment again, and it was something that she should allow herself to savour. The taste of a cocktail and Gabriel's dark eyes. She took another sip, and felt the effect of both going straight to her head.

'Let me mix something for you.'

Clara looked wonderful. Most women had at least one little black dress in their wardrobe, and many of the women tonight had opted for a variation on that theme. Clara's was quite plain, and beautifully cut so that it took nothing away from her curves. Her hair was caught back in a loose chignon, its colour the only lift that her outfit needed. If her aim was to blend into the background, she'd failed miserably.

She brushed past him, surveyed the rows of bottles carefully. The touch of her bare arm against the back of his hand and the trace of her scent was enough to send all his senses into overdrive. Less was very definitely more.

'I think…something smooth, but with a touch of bite. Stirred, not shaken?'

'Sounds good.' Forget shaken. He was definitely stirred.

She reached for bottles of rye whiskey and vermouth and Gabriel smiled. Clara was going to make a dry Manhattan, the way he liked it.

'Shall we go and sit down?' She nodded and he picked up the drinks, walking past the sitting room and leading her up the stairs.

He flipped the light on in his study, kicking the door closed before he set the drinks down. Clara sat in an armchair, slipping off her shoes and then reaching for her glass.

This was nice. And knowing that there were no cameras lent an intimacy to it all. 'So where did you learn to mix a cocktail? Is it a required skill for security work?'

'No. When I left the army I filled in working at a cocktail bar for six weeks. Then I got this job.'

'You never thought about going back to being a paramedic?'

'Briefly. But I wanted a change. And I found that I was good at this.'

'It must get pretty boring sometimes, following people around.'

'You think that you're boring?' She took a sip of her drink, quiet mischief dancing in her eyes.

'I didn't mean me. Following *other* people around.'

'Ah. Well, yes, *other* people can be boring at times. But we have such a wide range of clients. Families with children. People who are being stalked or threatened. My job isn't just about helping them to be safe, it's helping them to feel safe as well. We all need a sense of security.'

'I can identify with that. Although if a random stranger wants to put a dry Manhattan like this one into my hand, I might just take the risk and drink it.'

'Don't. I can always make you another. I stick to my recipes.' The warmth in her face and that light in her eyes calmed him. Gabriel felt more relaxed than he had in days.

'So you don't miss medicine?' The question had been bugging him since he'd seen her interest in Kaia's work. It must have taken a heavy blow to deflect someone with Clara's determination from her chosen career.

'I miss it. A lot sometimes…' She ran her finger around the rim of her glass, obviously wondering whether she should elaborate.

The party was over, and they were alone. Drinking cocktails. If this wasn't the time for talking then he didn't know what was.

'It's midnight. And you're off the clock.' Gabriel took his dinner jacket off and loosened his tie, to emphasise the point.

The way she looked him up and down made the tips of his fingers tingle. 'I suppose so.'

'So what made you change direction so suddenly?'

'Because… I'd lost my way. I couldn't go back and the only way was through. Medicine was my first love, but this is a very good second best.'

Her sudden honesty made Gabriel's stomach lurch. It felt as if they were on the edge of a precipice. A step back would be easy to take and a step forward would plunge them into the sweet unknown, where two people, talking after a party, might come to understand each other.

'So how does a woman like you get to lose her way?'

Clara had walked straight into this. Willingly. In truth, she'd practically galloped into it. Making cocktails together, following him upstairs so they could sit somewhere out of a camera's field of vision.

'It's a long story…'

'I've got all night.'

Clara swallowed hard. She was absolutely sure that Gabriel could think of many things that would take *all night.* But talking couldn't hurt.

'I wanted to work in medicine right from when I was little. I used to watch all the TV shows… you know, hero doctors and nurses. I decided I wanted to be a paramedic.'

'Bit more outdoorsy?' Gabriel's mouth twitched into a smile. 'And you're on the front line.'

She liked it that he knew that about her. 'Yes. I went to university, and when I was there I joined the army reserves.'

'Which was also outdoorsy and on the front line.'

'Stop making me sound so predictable. Yes, it was. I made some good friends there and I loved it. I graduated and went on to train with the London Ambulance Service. My best friend from the army reserve joined the regular army, and we had a flat together in London. I lived there all the time, and it was her base to come home to when she was on leave.'

'It sounds like a good life. Lots of possibilities…' There was a sudden sadness in Gabriel's voice. As if his own life, his family's wealth and his own talents had somehow left him with fewer possibilities.

But he seemed to shake off whatever he was feeling, taking a sip of his drink and nodding her on.

'I started seeing a guy I worked with…'

'Was he nice?' Something flickered at the side of Gabriel's eye.

'Yes, of course he was nice.' Clara gave him an eye-roll. 'What, you think I date creatures from the Black Lagoon?'

'Just asking. Go on.'

'And…things went well. Because he was nice.'

Clara flashed Gabriel a firm look to settle the question. 'He always knew that I was with the Territorials and he seemed fine with the idea that I'd be called up sooner or later. The timing wasn't great for us, it was two months after we got married. Tim wanted me to try to get out of it.'

'But you thought it was your duty to go.'

Gabriel already knew that she had gone. But all the same the feeling that he understood her motives trickled pleasurably down her spine.

'Yes, I did. My friend Steph had been killed in a bomb blast just a few months before that. I'd wanted her to be my bridesmaid, I'd even changed the date of the wedding to coincide with the end of her tour of duty, but she never made it.'

'So you *had* to go.' His eyes were suddenly dark, and Clara shot him a querying look. 'Sometimes the dead place more expectations on us than the living.'

'I never thought about it like that. But, yes, you're right, I did have to go. Tim accepted it and...the tour of duty for a reservist is usually six months but that often extends to a year. I was away for eleven months, and when I got back... let's just say that Tim had been lonely.'

'I assume you mean he'd done something about that?' Gabriel turned the corners of his mouth down in disapproval.

'Yes. I arrived home two days early at six in the morning. I was looking forward to taking a shower and getting into bed with him, but…my place had been taken.'

'He betrayed you.' Gabriel said the words without emotion, but there was no lack of empathy in his gaze.

'In more ways than one. Sandra was my friend before Tim even knew her. We all worked together.'

Gabriel's lip curled. 'So you ripped his arms off… I hope?'

Clara smiled without humour. 'No. I felt like giving it a go, but one thing you're taught when you learn to use force is that it's a last resort. Always. So I just walked out of the house and didn't go back. I resigned from my job as well. Working with both of them was…'

'More than anyone could be expected to do.'

'My parents went through a very bitter divorce when I was a kid. I spent most of my childhood being shunted back and forth between them, with each of them trying to turn me against the other.

When I left for university, it was such a relief to be able to make up my own mind where I was going to be. I was so determined that I wanted something different out of my marriage, but it turned out not to be so different after all.'

'And so you went back to the army?'

'I wanted the feeling of belonging that it gave me. I volunteered for another tour of duty, and at the time they needed medical personnel so they took me back for another year. I guess you could say that I just ran away.'

'You were with people who understood your values. And what those values can cost you. Like Mike does.'

Clara swallowed hard. Gabriel saw a lot more than she'd bargained for, and it was…comforting. 'That second tour gave me back the confidence to succeed. I looked around for a new job, something my experience might fit me for, and found Gladstone and Sullivan Securities. They've been good to me, and I really care about my job.'

'But it's not your first choice?'

'First choices don't take account of what life takes away from you.'

Gabriel nodded quietly, glancing at his watch. 'Yes. That's something I've learned too. But it's late and perhaps that's a story for another night, if I can persuade you to join me for a nightcap again?'

The question raised more questions. Whether midnight, which was theoretically beyond the hours of Clara's working day, and Gabriel's study, which was beyond the reach of the cameras, made any difference to their relationship. Strictly speaking, they didn't, but somehow it felt very different. And whether it might happen again. Saying *yes* now would open up those possibilities.

'Yes…maybe… I really should be getting home now, though.'

'I'll call you a taxi. Or you can always take the spare room for tonight.'

'Thanks. I should go home.'

He nodded, seeming to understand that as well. Clara slipped her shoes back on, watching as Gabriel thrust his arms back into his jacket. As if they were getting ready to face the real world again.

'I'd like to go running in the morning. Or the gym, if that's easier for you? I'm starting to miss the exercise.'

'Yes, of course. I can arrange for someone to

go with you. Or…would you like to come to *my* gym? They have training rooms, where I can teach you that arm lock, if you want to learn.'

'And it's more secure?' He grinned at her.

'It's local to Gladstone and Sullivan Securities. They know us there, so I'll be able to pin you to the floor without anyone rushing in to save you.'

Gabriel threw back his head, laughing. 'Sounds delightful. I'll be ready whenever you are.'

Gabriel had allowed himself a lie-in and stayed in bed until nine next morning. It seemed that Clara had too, and instead of her customary eight o'clock arrival, she'd called to say that she'd be there to pick him up at ten.

Gabriel looked at his phone. This was the first time that Clara had called him directly, rather than routing all their communications through the team. He wondered whether he might add her number to his contacts list and decided that he should. *Clara Holt.* Perhaps he'd also delete everyone else who appeared under 'C'…

That would be a step too far. Gabriel put his phone into his pocket and went upstairs to change. As expected, Clara arrived on the dot of ten, as fresh as the morning dew that they'd both slept through. A cool, sweet taste that he longed to feel on his lips.

But he'd promised that midnight was a time apart from everything else, and so he neglected to say that she looked particularly appealing, in her leggings and sweatshirt. Their conversation, as the car wound through the London streets, was wholly appropriate and centred mainly around the weather and the rules of Ronnie's Gym. It seemed that there was only one, which stated that Ronnie's word was law.

The gym was in one of the newly gentrified areas of the East End, an old building that had undergone a process of cleaning and renovation. The arched windows on the ground floor revealed a gleaming interior fitted out with exercise bikes, some of which were being used. Gabriel had expected something a little more no-nonsense.

The receptionist seemed to know Clara, and opened a combination locked door behind her. Clara led the way up an enclosed staircase, whitewashed bricks on either side.

The first floor was a little more as Gabriel had expected. Scrupulously clean, but without the exercise technology and bright colours of the ground floor. They passed a brick arch, which revealed an array of punchbags and a boxing ring, and Clara knocked on the open door of an office.

'Cupcake!' The woman inside rose. 'How are you?'

Gabriel fought to keep his face straight. He had no idea what Clara might do to him if he called her *Cupcake.* But the diminutive, middle-aged woman, dressed in a spotless pink polo shirt and dark blue sweatpants, seemed to have earned that right.

'I'm good, Ronnie. How are you?'

'Business is good. My son's getting married in the autumn. What's not to like?' Ronnie craned her neck to give Gabriel an assessing stare.

'This is Gabriel. Gabriel, this is Ronnie.'

Ronnie held out her hand, gripping his with a firm hold. He smiled and Ronnie beamed back at him. Apparently his first name was all that Ronnie required and the presence of one of Clara's team, standing behind them, didn't need to be questioned.

'Don't let her fool you.' Ronnie leaned towards him. 'Clara's got more up her sleeve than just her handkerchief.'

'Yes. She's already made that very clear…' His

answer seemed to be the correct one, and Ronnie chuckled, turning away and handing Clara a key from her desk.

'Here you are. I'll put the kettle on for Joe.'

'Thanks, Ronnie.' Clara seemed to have no reservations about leaving the guard behind to drink tea with Ronnie, and this was clearly a safe place. If anyone was going to do him any damage it was Clara. And that damage would be confined to his pride, and maybe his heart.

Clara led him along a whitewashed corridor, unlocking a bright, clean room, equipped with punch-bags at one end and a large practice mat, which took up most of the rest of the space. High arched windows were of obscure glass that let the light in but allowed privacy from the surrounding buildings.

'Ronnie seems pretty used to you bringing people here.'

'She looks after us.' Clara locked the door, stripping off her sweatshirt to reveal a body-hugging, sleeveless top.

'She built all this up herself?' Gabriel followed Clara's example, unlacing his gym shoes and taking his sweatshirt off.

'No. The first gym was purely a boxing gym,

on the first floor above a pub. That was her grandfather Ronnie. Her father Ronnie moved here when places like this went for a song. Ronnie's older brother was called Ronald, but he decided he wanted to be an accountant. Fortunately the old man's back-up plan was to call his daughter Veronica.'

'So this place has a bit of history attached to it.'

'Yes, loads. Ask Ronnie to show you her wall of photographs, if you've got a couple of hours to spare. A lot of the boxers who came out of the East End in the sixties went through here.'

'Maybe my father's heard of this place…' He knew little enough about his father's childhood and the thought suddenly interested him.

'Your father?' Clara shot him a questioning look.

'Yes, he was born in the East End—my grandparents came here after they were married. He took a course in pharmacy at the London University, and then went back to Italy to work in my uncle's chemist shop. From there he founded DeMarco Pharmaceuticals.'

'That's a real achievement. You must be proud.'

Pride didn't really play a role. Duty did, and the tearing feeling that he had to make the loss of their elder son up to his parents was Gabriel's first impulse. But Clara was right, he *should* be proud.

'Yes. He's achieved a lot. A great deal more than I have.'

'Well, I suppose you'd be hard put to get any richer. You've given yourself other challenges, though.' She folded her sweatshirt, putting it in a neat pile with her trainers in the corner of the room. 'I was wondering how your English was so good.'

'At home, my father spoke English and my mother spoke Italian.' That was the way that Gabriel had always viewed the two languages. Italian was the language of love, and English the language of duty.

She nodded, leading him onto the practice mat and facing him. 'Okay, so there are a few rules here. I won't go into all of them, since this isn't a formal lesson, but the main tenets are things you probably already know. Treat your opponent with respect. Use only the minimum amount of force required. Never act in anger.'

'Okay. Got it.'

'Really?' She looked up at him, her face luminous. 'It's an easy enough principle here, between the two of us. But can you extend that to the people we're dealing with now, who might put your family and friends at risk?'

Anger flooded through him. The idea of treating those opponents with respect was a little more difficult. 'Honestly? I'd find that… difficult.'

He was trembling. Gabriel had thought that today was just a bit of fun, a curiosity. But he was in deeper than he'd imagined, and Clara was using just the same techniques that he used on his patients to get them to face their feelings.

'That's fair enough, we're all human. But perhaps a little Zen is something to aim for. Shall we do some warming-up exercises?'

The warming-up exercises were more like simmering-down ones. When they'd finished, Gabriel felt more able to face his own anger and deal with it. When they graduated to a few basic self-defence moves, they seemed almost like a complex puzzle. Gabriel was stronger and bulkier than Clara, but she was fast and had a way of catching him off balance.

'Ready to try the hammer lock? It's not something I'd usually try this soon, but since you're a doctor I'm trusting you to know exactly how far to go before you hurt me.'

'I won't hurt you.' He couldn't.

Clara nodded, showing him the technique first and then asking him to try it. He carefully wound his arm around hers, his fingertips touching her bicep.

'Bit firmer than that. I can get out of that really easily.'

Gingerly, he curled his fingers around her arm, feeling the muscle flex at his touch. Making sure that he didn't extend her arm back to the point of any pain, he followed her instructions, tipping her forward onto her knees.

'That's it. You're still give me quite a bit of room to manoeuvre.'

'That can't be helped. I'm not going any further, I've reached my limit.'

'Fair enough, we all have them. But in the real world it's good to remember that the female of the species can be deadlier than the male.'

'Oh, I know that all right. Down a little further?'

'Yes. Don't push me, just apply leverage.'

Carefully Gabriel moved her down onto the mat. As if he were moving a patient almost, using his knowledge of the body to move her without doing any harm.

'That's good. Now, if you wanted, you could use your foot to keep my shoulder down and reach across with your hand to the other shoulder.'

That sounded a bit complicated and it was further than he wanted to go. Gabriel loosened his grip, releasing her and sitting back on the mat. 'I'll stop there, I think.'

She nodded, getting to her feet, holding her hand out to help him up. When he took it, she twisted suddenly, and he was on his back on the mat, her weight on top of him. That was okay. Better than okay, in fact. She was using her whole body to subdue his, and that involved physical contact. Quite a bit of it.

'The next lesson is always to keep an eye on your opponent. They might not be as gentlemanly as you are.'

'Yeah. Lesson learned.'

He relaxed, stretching beneath her as much as he could. She was good, and no doubt if she'd been using her full strength he'd be hurting right now. But instead of consolidating her advantage, she let go of one of his arms. Gabriel reached up, brushing his fingers against her cheek, and suddenly she smiled. Not that composed smile that she'd given him up till now but something full of warmth that seemed to glisten with a touch of mischief. She took his breath away.

The game had changed. Using all his strength, Gabriel rolled her over, ending up on top of her. The moves seemed more like loving than fighting. Two bodies locked together, testing each other's strengths and weaknesses. By now they'd probably have tumbled off the bed onto the floor, and he'd be so deep inside her…

'Oof!' His breath was suddenly pushed from his lungs as his back hit the mat, and Clara gained the upper hand again. That served him right for letting his mind wander. But the smile on her face, the lock of hair that had come unhooked from the elastic band that held it back were making that very difficult.

'You win, Clara.' He murmured the words and saw her eyes darken suddenly, her body still against his. What she would have done next was left to his imagination because a sudden banging at the door interrupted them.

'Open up, Cupcake.' That had to be Ronnie.

Clara jumped to her feet as if someone had just

put a handful of ice down her back, leaving Gabriel to sit up. Twisting the key in the lock, she opened the door.

'What's up, Ronnie?'

'Terry was doing some pad work with one of his lads, and the kid got him off balance and knocked him over. He's cut himself pretty badly, there's a lot of blood…'

'Okay, we'll come and take a look at him. Gabriel's a doctor.'

'Thanks.' Ronnie gave Gabriel a tight smile as he got to his feet, shaking his head in an attempt to knock some sense back into it. 'I'd really appreciate it.'

CHAPTER NINE

IT WAS JUST as well that Ronnie had knocked on the door when she did. Clara had felt Gabriel's body respond to hers and things had changed so suddenly that she was still reeling from the impact of it. She'd wanted him so very badly that it had almost made her forget that it broke every professional rule there was.

She pulled her shoes on, glancing at Gabriel. He flashed her a grin and she breathed a sigh of relief. It seemed that things were okay between them, and all she needed to do now was to avoid being alone in the same room as him. Easy.

When she led him through to the sparring area, she saw an older man, who she recognised by sight, sitting on a bench. Blood was running down his arm and pooling onto the floor and a couple of the gym staff were unsuccessfully trying to staunch it.

'All right, people. Give the doctor some room.' Ronnie addressed no one in particular and the little circle of people around Terry sprang back. Gabriel took a pair of surgical gloves from the first-aid kit, which lay open on the floor, and started to inspect Terry's shoulder.

'This doesn't look so bad, Terry.' Gabriel's words were reassuring, but something in his face told Clara that he wasn't happy with the situation. Without being asked, she fetched a pair of scissors from the first-aid box, so that Gabriel could cut away a little more of Terry's polo shirt to inspect the damage.

'Thanks…' He flashed her a smile. 'Are there some large dressing pads in there?'

Only about a hundred. Ronnie didn't do anything by halves when it came to looking after her patrons, and the first-aid kit was very well stocked. Clara took a pair of gloves from the box, pulling them on and fetching a handful of dressings.

'Take a look.' Gabriel turned to her. 'Can you see something I can't?'

The cut was three inches long and seemed relatively superficial. But blood was welling from it as if it were a deep wound. Clara looked up at Gabriel, shaking her head silently. It shouldn't be bleeding that much.

'Are you taking any medication, Terry? Blood thinners or anti-coagulants, anything like that?' Gabriel asked the obvious next question.

'No. Thanks, Doc, but I dare say it'll be all right in a minute. If you can just tape it up for me…'

'You're sure. Aspirin, even?'

'Nothing.' Terry's lips formed a hard line.

'All right.' Gabriel got to his feet. 'Clara, would you apply some pressure to the wound, please, see if you can stop the bleeding. Ronnie, I think the lad over there needs a few words from you. Looks as if he's feeling responsible for this.'

Clara glanced over her shoulder, and saw one of the young fighters from the boxing club sitting on the edge of the boxing ring, his head in his hands. It was a kind thought on Gabriel's part, but it didn't seem medically necessary right now.

'Right you are, Doctor,' Ronnie responded, walking over to sit next to the lad and put her arm around his shoulders. As soon as she turned her back, Gabriel bent down again.

'These are all your lads?'

'Yep. I run a club for teenagers.'

Gabriel nodded. 'It's a worthwhile thing to do. I imagine that Ronnie wouldn't let you into the ring to train them if you were taking anticoagulants.'

Of course! Gabriel wasn't just passing the time of day, he'd seen the situation and was dealing with it, quietly and firmly. Getting Ronnie out of the way was likely to loosen Terry's tongue a bit.

'Thing is, the way that cut's bleeding is of some concern to me. I need to know why, and there's a whole barrage of tests I'd have to prescribe—'

'Warfarin.' Terry could see the way this was going and capitulated suddenly. 'Two hundred milligrams a day.'

'Okay, thanks.' Gabriel nodded, his face showing no hint of the frustration he must feel. 'Has your diet changed at all recently? Been on holiday?'

'Yes, I'm just back. Me and the wife went to Italy. I've put on a few pounds, the food was great.'

'And your normal diet is pretty healthy, I imagine, you're in good shape. You eat plenty of vegetables?'

'Yes. When I go on holiday I take a bit of a break from my diet. For two weeks in the summer and a week at Christmas I get to eat whatever I like.'

'Did your doctor tell you that your diet can affect your INR level? Some leafy vegetables that are high in vitamin K can inhibit the effects of warfarin, so if your normal diet contains a lot of things like spinach and kale and you stop eating those things for a while, it'll affect how much warfarin you need to take.'

Terry grimaced, shaking his head. 'Maybe he said something about it. I…don't know. I was so cut up about it, because I knew that Ronnie would stop me from training the kids here. I've been doing it for twenty years…'

'Okay. I can see that this is important to you, and I'm sorry to have to say this, but contact sports really aren't advisable when you're on warfarin.'

'Yeah. I knew it wasn't too smart.' Terry's voice was heavy with resignation. 'Don't suppose you could talk to Ronnie for me, could you, Doc?'

'I can tell her what's happened if you want me to, but I won't tell her that it's okay for you to continue in the ring. I'm sorry, but it isn't.'

'Yeah, I know. Just give her the news, eh?'

'All right.' Gabriel's gaze flipped towards Clara. 'How are you doing there?'

'When I keep the pressure up it stops the bleeding.' She peeled up the corner of the dressing pad to inspect the edge of the cut. 'But it's not coagulating yet.'

'Okay. We'll need to take you to the hospital, Terry. They'll either seal the wound, or give you a shot to counteract the effects of the warfarin.' Gabriel got to his feet. 'And I'll go and have a word with Ronnie.'

Both she and Terry watched as Gabriel drew Ronnie to one side, talking to her quietly.

'I think the doc's calming her down…' Terry seemed to be clutching at straws.

'Um…yes. Maybe.' Clara saw Ronnie throw up her hand in a gesture of exasperation, and Gabriel blocked her path, standing between her and Terry. He was capable of charming the birds out of the trees, but Ronnie was a much more daunting prospect and it still remained to be seen whether Gabriel was going to succeed in smoothing things over.

Ronnie was nodding, and then turned, marching over towards them. Terry straightened a little, as if he was preparing himself for the onslaught.

'You damned fool, Terry Jarvis. Why didn't you tell me?'

'Sorry, Ronnie.' Terry had clearly decided that the less he said the better.

'So you should be. You think I'm going to let those boys lounge about in bus shelters when they could be in here, doing something useful? I'll get some of the lads to come and spar with them, and you can stay out of the ring. Right?'

'Right. Thanks, Ronnie.'

'Don't thank *me*. You know full well those kids need you, and I'm not having you bleeding to death on my premises. The doctor's giving me some written guidelines about what you can and can't do, and I'll be keeping my eye on you.'

Gabriel had followed her over, grinning broadly. 'Well, if that's settled, can we go to the hospital now?'

Ronnie turned on him, beaming. 'Just a tick, Doctor. I'll go and get my jacket and car keys.'

'You don't need to come, Ronnie. I don't want to put you out.' Terry was looking a great deal happier now, obviously content to take the sharp edge of Ronnie's tongue in return for the survival of his beloved boxing club.

'Someone needs to make sure you're all right,

you don't seem to be making much of a job of it.' Ronnie spun on her heel, clearly not in a mood to take any further disagreement, and made for her office.

'So, Doctor,' Clara murmured to him as he carefully took over the pressure on Terry's wound to allow her to brief her team for the departure. 'Seems as if you've found Ronnie's good side.'

He gave her a melting look that turned her insides to jelly. 'Looks as if I have, Cupcake.'

Every time they got too close, Clara took a step back again. For the last three days her manner had given no clue that he was anything other than a client. But Gabriel waited and finally she came to him. He was sitting in an armchair in his study, the door open as it had been for the last few nights. Just when he was beginning to feel that this was foolish, Clara appeared in the doorway, a glass in her hand.

'I thought you might like a nightcap.'

'Won't you join me? Or if you're driving tonight, then coffee.' He gestured towards the coffee machine in the corner behind his desk. As soon as she stepped over the threshold she was his. Away from the cameras and alone. She knew that as well as he did.

'Coffee would be nice, thank you.' She walked inside, closing the door behind her. Setting the drink down on the table in front of his chair, she sat down opposite, slipping off her sandals and tucking her legs up underneath her.

Way to go. Gabriel made the coffee and sat down. 'What's this?' He reckoned he knew the smell of rum and nutmeg that had followed her into the room.

The hint of the smile that he'd been wanting so badly hovered on her lips. Not the everyday one, which she bandied around without a thought. The one that, in his dreams, was reserved for him. Gabriel picked up the glass and tasted it.

'Rum Flip. And a good one. That's just the right amount of nutmeg.'

'I measured it, I'm afraid.'

Gabriel grinned. 'That works. Each to their own.'

She curled her hands around her coffee cup, and drank. This time was too precious to spend in silence, and when Gabriel opened his mouth to say something she did too.

'You first.' Gabriel smiled at her.

'I was just going to say that I've come to see how you're doing.'

'Fine. All in one piece still.' Gabriel deliberately misunderstood the question and she gave him a gentle chiding look.

'I meant how you were feeling.'

'I feel… I think it's probably best to just get on with things. Stay busy.'

'That's one way of doing it. You've been busy enough over the last few days.' Her gaze seemed to penetrate the minutiae of his life, right through to the most primal feelings. Fear. Passion. Guilt.

'I doubt there's much I can tell you about twelve-hour days that you don't already know.'

She thought for a moment. 'That's fair, I suppose. But, then, you know what drives me. I don't have much of a personal life and my work is the thing I know I can depend on.'

And now she was asking what drove Gabriel. He'd promised her that this was a story for another night, and now that night was here he couldn't let go of it. For the first time in a very long time, maybe ever, he didn't just want a woman's company, he wanted her to understand him.

'I guess…losing my brother made me feel that

I should live for both of us.' Gabriel took a sip of his drink, feeling the warmth begin to loosen his tongue.

'And work towards preventing other families from going through what yours has?'

'Yes. I don't have much time left, though. My father's going to be retiring soon, and when he does I'll be managing the family's interest in his company. It won't leave me as much time to devote to the charity.'

'And that's not what you want?'

'No, it isn't. I want to continue being a doctor and working with The Watchlight Trust.'

Clara was looking at him gravely. As if there were things that should be said but she wasn't sure what his reaction would be. Gabriel shrugged.

'Go on. You can ask.'

She nodded slowly. 'Why would you do that, Gabriel? Spend the rest of your life doing a job that you don't want to do, when you already have one that you want to do very much?'

'My father hasn't got anyone else to pass the company on to. We have a few personal differences—quite a lot of them actually—but we share the same values. He wants to see the company thrive and he feels that I'm a safe pair of hands.'

'And you haven't told him that you don't want to do this?'

'If I do, he'll just keep working. I want him to retire and for my parents to have some time together—they deserve it. And it's my duty. They lost a son and I can't ever make it up to them but… I can do this.'

Clara frowned. 'I'm just wondering why you think you have to make things up to your parents.'

'*I* was the reason that Pietro was in the cave. It was a local beauty spot, full of mineral deposits and unusual rock formations, and I wanted to see them. My mother wouldn't let me go alone, because it's cut off by the tide every afternoon, and so Pietro said he and his friends would take me. I was only eleven, and they were all seventeen, so I thought I was a pretty cool guy to be tagging along with them.'

'That doesn't make it your fault.'

There was more. Things he hadn't told anyone. But Clara specialised in safe places, and the warmth of her gaze told him that maybe, after all these years, this was a safe place for him to go after all.

'There were two rock falls. Pietro was walking ahead of me and he escaped the first collapse completely. He came back to dig me out, along with one of his friends who'd been right next to me and was badly hurt. Pietro cleared his mouth and made sure that he was breathing, and managed to stop the bleeding.'

'That's pretty good for a seventeen-year-old. The first things I'd check.'

Gabriel smiled. It meant something that Clara had said that, even though he'd thought it many times before.

'Pietro was really calm, and he was telling us all that things would be all right and that someone would come and get us. He looked at my leg, I'd hurt my ankle when I fell and he put a makeshift splint on it and bound it up with his windcheater. I remember him tying the sleeves into a knot…'

It was the little things that always seemed to hurt the worst. The way that Pietro had drawn a smiley face in the dust. Seeing his mother's fingers tremble as she'd touched her son's coffin.

But the story deserved an ending. Clara was sitting quietly, waiting.

'When the second rock fall came, there was this awful rumbling, groaning sound at first. Pietro picked me up and carried me back into a second cave that was situated behind the first. Then he went back…' Gabriel heard his voice crack and struggled to regain control. 'He and his friends were all buried. There was nothing I could do. I tried to dig for them, but the rocks were too big for me to move.'

'And you were there for three days.' Gabriel could see tears glistening in her eyes.

'They had to sink a borehole into the cave, the mouth was completely blocked. The only thing that got me through it was that I wanted to tell everyone that my brother had been a hero.'

'It's more than any child should have to go through, Gabriel.' She looked down at her cup, swirling the dregs of her coffee thoughtfully. 'You were a hero too.'

'No.' The idea was impossible. 'I was just a scared kid and I couldn't do anything.'

'You survived. You grew up and now you're supporting people who try to help others, the way your brother did.'

It was nice to hear, even if Gabriel wasn't convinced that Clara had it right. 'Or I'm just someone trying to fill my brother's shoes. Not all that well most of the time. Take your pick.'

Clara grimaced at him. 'I know what I think.'

So did he. For some reason, Clara always thought the best of him, even though he hadn't given her much reason to do so. They sat in companionable silence as Gabriel finished his drink, and then Clara flashed him a smile.

'I'll take these downstairs and put them in the dishwasher.' She put on her sandals, picking up the glass and her cup. 'Thank you. For talking.'

'Thank you for listening.' They were slipping back into their everyday routine. The one where Clara followed him, watching but never reacting. Suddenly Gabriel couldn't bear it. He took the crockery from her hands, putting it back down on the table, and moved to the door, leaning his back against it.

'I'm taking it for granted that you'll be able to get past me in a second if you want to…'

She nodded slowly, taking a step towards him. 'That's a fair assumption.'

'And this…' He let his fingers trace her cheek. 'If you don't want this?'

'It would be a fair assumption that I'd move away.' She stood stock still, looking up at him. Suddenly all the reasons why he shouldn't do this didn't matter.

Clara had told herself that she'd come up here because she wanted to find out more about what made Gabriel tick. That she wanted to be able to do her job better. But watching him for days, staying impassive and uninvolved, had been an exercise in self-restraint and longing. She was here because she wanted be alone with him.

She felt his arm coil around her waist, and he pulled her slowly against him. Breathing in each moment and making it last, in the dark warmth of his eyes. She could feel his arousal and if he couldn't feel her instinctive response then he was made out of stone.

His lips curved into a smile. 'I've been thinking about this moment ever since I met you.'

'I know. You mentioned it at the time, remember?'

'Not entirely. I know what I was thinking but I can't remember what I said. I was suffering from a lack of impulse control.'

'Funny you should say that. So am I.' Clara

knew that she shouldn't do this. But she couldn't help it. Touching him now, feeling his touch, seemed more important than anything else.

Just one kiss. Something that would satisfy her curiosity and never be repeated. Where was the harm in that?

She had to stand on her toes to kiss him, and when she did, warmth exploded through her. Gabriel's response was tender, and full of the longing that she felt for him.

'I'm trying to find the words to tell you how beautiful you are…' He slid one hand into her hair, pushing it back so that he could trail kisses along her neck. 'Might take a while. There are many, many words to describe you…'

'Take your time.' He could take all the time he wanted, to do all the things *she* wanted. Clara let her fingers explore the strong curve of his arms and shoulders, and the muscles flexed beneath her touch.

He kissed her again, tenderness morphing into something stronger and more demanding. The last time she had been here she'd brought him to his knees, and tonight he was more than repaying her.

'Clara…' He whispered her name, and the

feel of his breath on her neck made her tremble. Slowly he drew back, trapping her in the heat of his gaze.

'You're exquisite. Beautiful and strong, and…' He quirked his lips down. 'I want to spend all night telling you, but…'

The consequences of her actions hit home suddenly. She should have known that a kiss would never be enough for either of them. And she could lose her job for this, and then everything would come tumbling down. All she'd done to distance herself from a faithless husband and a childhood that had been scarred by insecurities.

Gabriel felt her shiver in his arms. Not the delicious tremor of excitement that his kiss had elicited but the kind of response that would have accompanied a sudden, icy wind blowing through the room. In that moment, he knew that he had to make this right.

'Clara, no one knows. There are no cameras…'

Panic flared in her eyes, and she pulled away from him. This was much harder and more confusing than giving in to his fantasies and kissing her.

'I know. You know.'

'And we both know that we're going to stop now. You'll stop because your professional integrity means a great deal to you. And I'll stop because I respect that and want you as a friend.'

She nodded, pressing her lips together. Gabriel had gone to every place imaginable with more women than he could remember, but this… He hadn't been here before. Knowing that, he had to let Clara go.

'It can't happen again, Gabriel. My job's at stake, and it's so important to me…'

'It's okay,' he reassured her. 'We won't let it.'

'So you'll forget all about this?'

'No. I want to remember that we talked, and that we kissed. And that then we drew a line under it, because we value each other's principles.'

She thought for a moment and then suddenly stretched up, kissing his cheek. The brief touch of her lips was more affecting than the most sensual caress.

'Thank you. I'd like that. I'm going to go now, before I'm tempted to kiss you again.'

'Good idea.' Gabriel moved away from the door, opening it for her. 'I'll see you in the morning?'

'Yes.' As she walked past him into the hallway, she seemed to remember something and turned back. 'I'm glad we're remembering it. It would be a crime to forget something that nice.'

He closed the door behind her, leaning back against it and closing his eyes. Gabriel's relationships generally went a little more predictably. Talk a little, smile a lot. A first kiss that could be a good night, or the beginning of a better one. And maybe, just maybe, after hours of love-making, that exquisite moment of togetherness, which allowed him to forget that he was a man who always felt himself alone. It came close to the kind of feeling he'd had with Clara tonight, but had none of the intensity of feeling himself tumble into her smile.

The outrageous idea that no-strings sex might be overrated crossed his mind. How many times had he walked away from an affair without looking back? But somehow Clara's touch seemed to linger, long after he'd heard the front door close and watched from the window as she walked to her car. It followed him from his study to his bedroom, the empty sheets seeming to mock him as he climbed into bed.

CHAPTER TEN

CLARA HADN'T SLEPT well last night. Thoughts of Gabriel's lips, trailing fire across her skin, vied with fears over whether she could trust him to keep silent about what had passed between them in the privacy of his study.

She arrived at his house and found him eating breakfast. As he offered her coffee, the warmth in his eyes told her all she needed to know. Gabriel regretted nothing, and he would say nothing.

His diary was, as always, full. A morning's work at the charity's offices, along with a visit to Mike, to make sure that he was ready for his journey up to Hertfordshire the next day. Clara followed him, sitting quietly on the edges of everything, but somehow his gaze seemed to find her every now and then.

The afternoon was taken up by therapy sessions at the clinic, and then back home to dress for a dinner party, while the security team took a break in the basement office.

'He won't be going yet, will he?' One of the guards who would be staying behind at the house tonight was new on the team. When Clara rose, collecting her handbag and pulling on her coat, barely fifteen minutes after she'd returned, he raised his eyebrows.

Clara looked at her watch. 'I'll give him…two minutes at most. What do you think, Ian?'

'I'll go for three. Three to four.'

'Five minutes.' Joe was watching the feeds from the cameras. 'He got as far as the top of the stairs and then went back into his bedroom. He's on the phone. Looks pretty intent over it…'

'Maybe we need two cars for tonight.' Guessing what a client might do next was a way of whiling away the time, but Ian was obviously thinking ahead as well. Clara felt an ache of dismay at the idea that Gabriel might be returning here with someone, and that her place next to him in the back of the SUV might be taken by another woman.

'I'll follow you, then.' If someone was going to have to make room for the lovebirds, then she'd take the second car.

'Okay.' Ian was studying the camera feed over Joe's shoulder. 'One minute thirty. Looks as if you won this one, Clara.'

Gabriel was standing in the front hall, his phone still pressed to his ear, waving at the camera in a signal that he was ready to go. Clara picked up the keys for the second SUV, and made her way upstairs.

He was listening on the phone, trying to fix his cufflinks at the same time. Even for someone as adept at doing two things at once as Gabriel was, it wasn't really working, and Clara held out her hand silently. He nodded his thanks, giving her the cufflinks.

'I'm not entirely sure, Mike. The idea is that you choose the sessions you feel might benefit you the most, and discuss that with the people there.' He grinned at Clara. Gabriel had said much the same thing to Mike that afternoon.

She caught Ian's silent glance in Joe's direction, and knew that the question of whether Gabriel was talking to his date for the night had been settled. All the same, a second car might not be a bad idea. It would establish a precedent.

Clara put the car keys into her pocket, and Gabriel held out one arm, still talking to Mike. 'No, mate. Look, maybe the best thing to do is plan to decide later. They'll give you plenty of time to think about it…'

He flashed Clara a frustrated look. Mike had wanted to know every detail of what was going to happen on the course, so that he could plan his reactions, and Gabriel had gently talked him out of it, but it seemed that Mike had now had second thoughts. Clara snapped the cufflink into place, and as Gabriel passed the phone from one hand to the other he almost dropped it.

'No, sorry. Still here. I'm just juggling my phone. Clara's just helping me with my cuff-links… Yeah, perks of having protection.' He looked up at Clara suddenly. 'Mike says hello.'

'Tell him hello back. And to do as he's told.' This felt suddenly intimate. Helping him with his cufflinks and sharing a phone conversation. Clara reminded herself that although Joe and Ian had gone to fetch the cars, they were still visible on camera.

'You heard the lady?' Gabriel grinned at her. 'Look, can you hold on for one minute, Mike? When I'm in the car we'll have plenty of time to talk. Yeah…one minute.'

He switched the phone to mute and nodded towards her car keys. 'You're not coming with us?'

'I'll be following in a second car.' Clara felt her cheeks begin to flush in response to his enquiring look. 'It gives us a backup, and you might want to give someone a lift back to town.'

'What do you think I am?' He got the unspoken reason straight away.

'A free agent.'

Suddenly all the warmth from last night flashed in his eyes. 'Yeah, okay. Well, as a free agent, I won't be giving anyone a lift back to town tonight. That's a firm intention.'

Despite herself, Clara couldn't help smiling. Ian wasn't always right. 'Well, two cars are better than one. I'll be right behind you.'

'Whatever you say. Make sure you're looking over my shoulder.' He gave her a delicious smile and raised the phone to his ear again. 'Mike… are you still there? Yeah, good. Now, about tomorrow…'

Gabriel appeared alone in the hallway with his host and hostess, bidding them goodnight and thanking them for the evening. He waited for Clara to call Joe to let him know they were ready to leave, flashing her an *I told you so* look before they walked outside.

It was a quiet night, the full moon hanging low in the sky and shedding an eerie light on the trees on either side of the road. A car, travelling at speed, approached from behind and Clara kept her eyes on the rear-view mirror as it slowed, falling into line behind them. Then, on a stretch of straight road, it overtook both SUVs and continued on into the distance. Just someone out for the night, who couldn't wait to get wherever they were going.

'Clara. Up ahead.' The walkie-talkie on the dashboard crackled into life.

'Yes, I see it.' A small bridge, most of the parapet on one side smashed. And in the stream below the car was upended, the nose in the water with the tail caught on the side of the bridge.

There was a procedure for this. Clara stopped the car, giving the leading SUV room to back up out of the way so that the client could be made safe. But it didn't move, and the back door swung open. Gabriel wasn't the average client and he clearly had other ideas.

'Get back into the car.' Clara ran over to him. 'I'll deal with this.'

'The hell you will. Not on your own.' Gabriel took off towards the riverbank, sliding down the steep slope.

Ian was already out of his seat, following Gabriel. Clara grabbed the tool kit from the back of the SUV, and ran after them, clambering down the muddy embankment. She could see now that the driver's door was slightly open and there was a woman in the passenger seat, desperately trying to free herself from her seat belt. Blood was pluming in the water around her, which rose and fell, almost submerging her when it reached its highest point.

Gabriel was trying to get the driver's door open far enough to reach into the car, but it was wedged tightly against something under the water. He waded around, tugging at the passenger door.

The tool bag was too heavy to carry into the water. Clara unzipped it, grabbing what she needed, and waded out towards the car, gasping at the icy cold of the stream. Now she could see that the driver's seat was empty.

'Ian, the driver's not here,' Clara called over to him. 'He might be hurt somewhere. Can you ask Joe to try and find him?'

Ian nodded, getting the message. If the driver wasn't hurt and this was all a set-up, then they needed to find him as well. But that was looking increasingly unlikely. Clara turned her attention to the car door. Brute force wasn't working, and maybe a little leverage would budge it. She inserted the end of the crowbar she'd brought with her between the door and the frame, pushing as hard as she could. The door didn't move, but when Gabriel added his weight to it, it shifted.

Gabriel pulled the door open, ducking inside the car to release the woman's seat belt. 'It's jammed. Have you got something to cut it with?'

Before she could hand him the knife, another rush of water submerged the woman, and Gabriel with her. Then both their heads broke the surface as Gabriel supported the woman's head above the water as best he could.

Clara squeezed past Gabriel to cut the seat belt, and he tried to lift the woman but her legs were trapped. Taking a deep breath, he ducked down into the water.

She was young, and she'd almost stopped struggling now, her head lolling to one side against the headrest. If Gabriel couldn't free her soon, she was going to drown.

Suddenly the water clouded again with blood, which was carried away by the stream. As Gabriel's head broke the surface, the woman floated free and Clara grabbed her, keeping her head above the water. Gabriel took a moment to catch his breath and then helped Clara to pull her out of the car.

Carefully, he carried her to the riverbank, climbing the muddy slope and setting the woman down on the blanket that Ian had laid on the ground at the top, in the shelter of one of the SUVs. Gabriel laid her down on her side, clearing her mouth and supporting her head, and the woman suddenly began to choke and retch.

Then she was still again, unresponsive but breathing. Gabriel reached for the first-aid kit that Ian had fetched from the boot of the SUV, and took out two pairs of gloves, handing one to Clara.

'Will you take a look at her legs, please, Clara? Ian, have you called an ambulance?' He was in charge now, no more following and waiting for the security team to do their jobs.

'Yes. They'll be here soon.'

'Thanks. Can we have some light here, please?'

Ian fetched a lantern, switching it on and setting it down beside Gabriel. Then he got into the driver's seat of the other SUV, turning it so that the headlights shone towards them.

'Great, thanks, Ian.' Gabriel glanced up at Clara. 'She's breathing and her pulse is steady. How do her legs look?'

'Right leg seems okay, but she's bleeding badly from a wound on her left leg.' Clara bent over, looking carefully. 'I can't see anything in it. I'm going to apply pressure.'

'All right, let me know if you need any help…'

They worked silently as Ian and Joe kept watch over them. Gabriel looked up as the murmur of a siren sounded in the distance. 'I hope that's on its way here…'

Suddenly the woman moved, groaning in pain. That was a good sign, Gabriel had obviously been worried about her apparent listlessness. He calmed her, holding her still, until the ambulance drew up on the other side of the bridge.

Clara stepped back, letting the ambulance crew take her place. Gabriel was still working, helping them to stabilise her before they took her to the hospital, and there was nothing more now that she could do. She stripped her gloves off, shivering in the night breeze.

More lights, this time those of a police car. Clara checked that Ian and Joe still had eyes on Gabriel and walked towards it, to speak with the police officer who had arrived to take charge of the scene. When she expressed her concerns about the second occupant of the car, she was told that he'd been found by another police car, less than a mile up the road.

'He went for help?' Clara put the best interpretation she could on the man's actions.

'I'll need to have a word with the young woman.' The policewoman quietly refused to give any more details. 'How is she?'

'You may have to wait awhile. The doctor's with her now, but she was almost drowned and she's lost a lot of blood from a wound on her leg.'

'Okay. Good thing he was here on the scene.' The policewoman looked at the two dark SUVs ruminatively. 'So what's your involvement…?'

Gabriel had satisfied himself that his patient was stable, and she was loaded into the back of the ambulance. Clara had given her name and contact details and promised that everyone would be available to give statements in the morning. Now she needed to get Gabriel home.

Ian quietly put a blanket around her shoulders, and Clara wrapped it around her thankfully. 'You want me to drive? You can go with Joe and Gabriel.'

'No, I'm okay.' Clara would rather snuggle into a blanket in the back seat of the other SUV. But that wasn't acceptable—her first priority was Gabriel's safety, and he was safer with Ian and Joe.

'All right.' Ian hesitated. 'We couldn't stop him from getting out of the car.'

'I know. Don't worry about it. Once Gabriel decides there's something he needs to do, there is no stopping him. All we can do is keep up, and you and Joe did a good job tonight. Let's just get him home.'

'Leave it with me. You just concentrate on getting yourself back.' Ian grinned at her, and walked back to the SUV.

Ian and Joe had done a good job, but Clara wasn't so sure about herself. Not being able to stop Gabriel was just an excuse. She'd known she couldn't and she hadn't wanted to, because the woman in the car might well have died without him.

Clara walked slowly to the car. She may have

failed to do her job tonight, but it felt so much more important that Gabriel had succeeded in doing his.

He had to know. Gabriel wasn't sure why he needed to know so badly but he did. When they arrived back at his home, he took a much-needed shower, allowing himself to luxuriate in the warm water, and then made the unprecedented step of asking Joe to send Clara up to his study as soon as she too had showered and got into some dry clothes.

When she knocked on the door, she waited for him to call her inside, and when she entered her hands were empty. No coffee or tea. No unexpected cocktails. Clara stayed on her feet until he waved her across to a seat.

'I was very thankful for your presence of mind tonight, in bringing the tools we needed so quickly…' He decided to start with the good part.

'We carry those tools for just such an eventuality.' She was in shut-down mode, giving him as little information as possible.

'You told me to get back into the car.'

She nodded. 'Yes, I did.'

'Why did you do that, Clara? I'm a doctor, you don't remove a doctor from the scene of an accident.'

'We have an established procedure for situations such as these.'

Anger rose in Gabriel's chest. 'We've been through this before. Stop trying to manage me. I need you to talk to me, right now.'

Clara thought for a moment, and the threat of disappointment began to loom. Then she puffed out a breath.

'In situations like these, we have to balance the likelihood of a genuine emergency with the possibility that an accident has been staged to draw you out, away from your protection. It happens, Gabriel. We have to secure your safety and then offer help.'

Gabriel almost couldn't bear to ask. Could Clara really have betrayed everything that he stood for—everything he'd thought she stood for—so easily?

'And that's what you were going to do?'

She stared at him for a moment, as if she didn't understand the question. Then she turned her head away. 'It's a hard decision to make, Gabriel.'

'Which is why it's so important to get it right.'

She glared at him, anger in her eyes. 'If you must know, I knew you wouldn't stay in the car, whatever I said. I was glad you didn't. Is that what you want to hear?'

Relief washed over him. 'That's exactly what I want to hear.'

'Well, it shouldn't be. My job is to protect you.' He could see the anguish in her eyes now. Clara had been faced with an impossible choice.

'And you *did* protect me. I believe it's worth taking a risk to save someone else, and you believe it too. If I let fear make me betray my principles, then I'm nothing. You'd have nothing left to protect.'

'You're thinking like a doctor, Gabriel. Which is okay, I suppose, because you *are* a doctor. I'm not an ambulance paramedic any more.'

He shrugged. 'If the cap fits…'

'No. Don't do that, Gabriel. You know why I gave up my job as a paramedic. And you know this job means a great deal to me, and I want to do it right.' She waved her hand, as if she just didn't want to think about it any longer. 'I suppose what's done is done.'

'Yes. And like it or not, I think you did the right thing. Virginia's going to be okay—'

'She told you her name was Virginia? I saw her talking to you as they were getting her ready to put her into the ambulance.' Clara's sudden flash of interest made Gabriel smile.

'Yes. She was in the car with her boss. He'd asked her out to a nice restaurant for dinner and she went with him. Apparently he's married...'

He saw understanding dawn in Clara's eyes. She'd clearly been wondering why the driver had left the scene so quickly.

'So she had a lucky escape. In more ways than one.'

'That's exactly what I told her. I said that there was someone out there who would treat her better than this and who would stick with her, whatever happened...' Gabriel frowned. He probably wasn't the one to give anyone relationship advice.

'That's fair.' The knowingness in Clara's eyes told him that she hadn't failed to see the incongruity of the situation.

'All right. Give me a break, eh?'

She smiled, getting to her feet. When she bent

towards him, brushing her lips against his cheek, he felt a little dizzy suddenly.

'You're one of the best, Gabriel. I'm going home now to get some sleep.'

He leaned back in his seat. They both knew that Clara had made the right decision, even if she wouldn't admit it. And they both knew that they'd made a good team. That meant a great deal more to Gabriel than it should.

CHAPTER ELEVEN

WHEN SHE RETURNED the following morning, she was smiling but distant again. As if she felt that their growing connection would compromise her ability to protect him. Clara was lost in the world of rules and procedures that she retreated to whenever she felt challenged by real life.

She followed him from one appointment to another, going through the now familiar routines that ensured his safety. And it went without saying that when Gabriel retreated to his study, there was no tap on his door, and no opportunity to talk on a more relaxed basis with her.

His days were, as always, hard work. He had patients to see, as well as his work at the charity. But the evenings were his own.

Gabriel started with dinner. Not alone and by candlelight, because Clara wouldn't have accepted that. But having her go with him to one of his favourite restaurants in London, to meet with the representatives of another charity that was working with PTSD patients, was a surprisingly good second best.

The two-man security detail had been stationed away from their table, but Clara had been persuaded to sit by his side. Dressed plainly, in a failed attempt not to stand out from the crowd, she picked at her food, alert to what was going on around them. But from time to time the faintest of smiles told him that she was also following the conversation and Gabriel wondered what she might add from her own experience if given the chance.

During the next week, his diary filled up spectacularly fast. People who were expecting a short meeting at his office suddenly found themselves switched to a lunch or dinner, where they could really get to know each other and talk about the issues. Everyone was happy, the business of the moment was conducted satisfactorily and in convivial surroundings, and Gabriel paid the bill from his own pocket, so as not to make a dent in the charity's modest entertainment budget. And he got to have Clara sitting by his side, instead of stationed outside a meeting room at the charity's offices.

'What do you think?' he asked, as the car back to his home manoeuvred deftly through the evening traffic.

'Me?' Clara feigned surprise, but it was obvious that she must think something about a project that sought to make working paramedics' lives a little safer.

'Yes. You've done the job, I haven't. You must think something. Or were you too busy watching everyone else in the room?'

'I think…they've got a lot of great ideas, but they're putting too much emphasis on reaction. How to get out of a dangerous situation, rather than avoiding it happening in the first place.'

Gabriel nodded. 'Yes, that's exactly what I was thinking. I don't suppose you'd be able to help me with this one? Write down a few main points that I might include in my response to their proposal that we join forces and work together.'

Clara flushed. That was exactly what he wanted her to do, because it betrayed the fact that she actually had been interested in what had been said around the table tonight. 'It's… I didn't really hear everything.'

'Really? I thought you had eyes in the back of your head, and that you could comfortably listen to four conversations at once.' He teased her a little.

'I have my limitations. It's only three conversations at once.' She smirked at him, and Gabriel felt a tingle run down his spine. He slid a copy of the paperwork that he'd been given across the car seat towards her.

'It's all in here.'

Clara's hand hovered over the folder, and then she shook her head. 'I don't think that's appropriate. It's been a while since I worked as a paramedic and… Another time, maybe.'

It was an excuse. That reprobate of a husband hadn't just taken Clara's ability to trust from her, he'd taken the job she'd loved as well. Gabriel wanted to protest, but Clara had made her decision and he had to respect that.

'It's okay if I ask again? Another time?' Maybe he could at least keep that option open.

She smiled suddenly. 'Yes. It's okay if you ask again.' They lapsed into silence for a while. 'Do you get tired of this? The social round?' She was looking out of the car window now, and the question came right out of the blue.

In truth? Yes, often. Gabriel's habit of keeping himself busy so that he could sleep at night sometimes grated on him. When he'd been at medical school, it had been his studies, and now he surrounded himself with people whenever he wasn't working.

'Sometimes. Why, are you tired of it already?'

'No. If I wasn't working I'd find it wonderful.' Gabriel reckoned that this was about as close as Clara was going to get to saying she'd enjoyed herself. 'I'm not sure I could keep it up for too long, though. I'll be needing a rest soon.'

'You haven't forgotten about Italy, have you? That's just over a week away and you'll have four days' rest then.'

'Yes. Just enough time for me to get bored with securing your house while you're away and start missing all of this.'

'Ah, so you'll miss me.' Gabriel had been hoping she might. 'I'll miss you too.'

'I didn't say I was going to miss *you.*' She shot him a smile. 'I'll miss being busy.'

It was a little too late for Clara to back-pedal now, they both knew what she'd meant. Gabriel thought about Clara when she wasn't there too. So much so that the idea of calling one of his women friends and asking if she'd like to spend an evening with him hadn't even occurred to him since he'd met Clara. Even if he had engineered the rendezvous to happen after she'd gone home, her scent would still have lingered. The thought of her. Gabriel put aside the disturbing idea that maybe he was losing his grip.

'Tomorrow evening's going to be a change. You like the opera?'

She gave him a guarded look, which was usually accompanied by telling him that what she thought was irrelevant. She could say it as much as she liked, it wasn't irrelevant to him.

'Do you normally dress up?'

'It's the opera. It's supposed to be sublime, and I can't abide this tendency just to come as you are for it. Grant and Sara Goodman are joining me and Sara will definitely be dressing up. We have a box in the Grand Circle.'

'Okay. I'll bring something that blends in.'

He chuckled. Maybe it was time to put this one to bed. 'Clara, you always look fabulous. You couldn't blend in if you tried.'

The look she gave him was almost a smile. 'Clearly I'll have to try a bit harder, then.'

Clara looked stunning. A red dress, the soft fabric following her curves like a caress. When he saw her, Gabriel caught his breath.

'Does this stand out enough for you?' She gave him a mischievous smile, and Gabriel felt a flush of satisfaction. She'd worn the dress to please him, and he just wished he could tell her how much he liked that idea.

'You look exquisite. The dress is lovely, too.'

She gave an amused wince and pretended to fan her cheeks with her hand. 'So charming.'

Was that a challenge? Gabriel was confident that he could deliver more than enough charm to drive Clara to distraction.

He helped her on with her coat, and tucked her hand into the crook of his elbow, leading her out to where the car was waiting for them. Good manners and attentiveness wore her down, and by the time he'd escorted her to her seat at the opera house, she'd had enough.

'Stop it, Gabriel.' She leaned towards him, tapping the back of his hand with the rose he'd given her. 'Or I'll forget I'm here to protect you and beat you to death with this rose.'

'That's not going to work. The thorns are shaved off so they don't scratch your hand.'

'Well, perhaps I can try strangling you with it, then.'

This was the Clara who made the blood rush to his head. The one who was more than a match for any compliment he could devise. 'I'll remember not to choose such a long stem in future. Are you saying that staring at you, instead of the stage, is out of the question?'

'Yes. I'm the one watching you, remember. You're here for the music.'

'Understood.' Gabriel settled back into his seat. Tonight promised to be as enjoyable as he'd hoped.

The opera had been wonderful. Grant and Sara had been friendly and accepting, and Clara had managed to survive the melting look in Gabriel's eyes, and the way his evening suit made him look so mouth-wateringly handsome. The music had been sublime and it had been a struggle to stay focused on what she was there for.

She lay in bed, the music still running in her head. Gabriel had seemed so much at one with it, obviously caring more for the performance than who he might see or be seen by. Yet another contradiction in a man who seemed defined by the unexpected.

Her phone rang and Clara sat bolt upright in bed, reaching for it. At this time of night, a call was generally some kind of emergency.

'Clara Holt.'

'Clara. It's Alistair Duvall. I'm sorry to call you so late but I think we have a…situation.'

'Where are you, Alistair? Are you all right?'

'Yes…yes… But I'm in my office. I popped back after an evening meeting to get something I need for tomorrow. There's no one here, and I didn't bother with the lights. I saw the screen on Gabriel's computer come on…'

'Okay.' Clara thought quickly. Gabriel's computer screen faced away from Alistair's office… 'Don't move. Can you see from where you're standing now if there's a red camera light?'

'Um…yes, I think so. I can see something like that reflected in the windows. Do you want me to go and switch it off?'

'I need you to make a decision. If you were to cut the power to your whole system then that would stop the intrusion right away, but if we allow whoever's in your system to keep going it would be easier to trace them. What do we do, Alistair?'

There was a moment's silence. 'All our patient notes are on the clinic's network, which is entirely separate, so they're safe. There are a few things that we'd prefer to keep out of the public domain, but it's nothing I can't handle. My primary concern is that what's happening to Gabriel is dealt with as soon as possible.'

'We'll do it, then? Let the intrusion continue in the hope we might trace it. There are no guarantees, Alistair.'

'Yes. We'll do it.'

'Okay, I want you to go back to the reception area right now, without switching on any of the lights or getting into the line of vision from the camera. I'll call the guard and tell him what's happening.'

'Right you are. What then?'

'I'll be on my way to Gabriel's in five minutes, just to make sure everything's okay there. I'll pop in to the office on my way.'

'Okay. I'll see you when you get here.' Alistair seemed to be taking all of this in his stride, replying as if she'd offered to drop round for coffee. Clara was already out of bed and pulling jeans and a sweatshirt out of her chest of drawers. So far the team working on who was behind the threats to Gabriel's family hadn't got very far. But this could be the break they'd been waiting for.

During the fifteen-minute drive, Clara had called the guards at Gabriel's house, and the leader of the technology team, getting him out of bed. She parked outside the office, looking for any signs of physical surveillance, before getting out of her car. Alistair was waiting for her in the reception area.

'Everything okay?' She addressed the guard, who nodded.

'The screen of Dr DeMarco's computer has gone blank now.'

'Right. The technical team's working on it, so just sit tight. You know you can always call for backup if you need it.'

'Yes. Would you like me to get someone to accompany Dr Duvall home?'

Clara nodded but then Alistair stepped in. 'That's not necessary. You're going over to Gabriel's place now, Clara?'

'Yes.'

'Would you like me to come with you? I won't be sleeping tonight until I know what's happened, and we may as well all stay awake together.'

Clara would be glad of Alistair's support. 'Thanks. Let's go, then.'

* * *

Gabriel had been woken by the night guards and the situation explained to him. As expected, he was in the kitchen, pacing like a caged lion.

'What's happening? Can you call and find out?'

'Calling the technical team isn't going to make them go any faster, Gabriel.' Clara tried to inject a note of calm. 'We should know one way or the other within the hour.'

'An hour!' The idea didn't seem to placate Gabriel at all.

'Oh, for goodness' sake, Gabriel. Stop pacing or you'll wear a furrow in the floor. I'll make some coffee. I think we could all do with some.'

Alistair started to fiddle with the coffee machine and Gabriel threw himself into a chair. Even Clara's nerves were beginning to wear a little thin. This meant so much to Gabriel and the thought that someone had attacked the charity because of him must be tearing him to pieces.

It was forty-five minutes before her phone rang. Silence fell around the kitchen table and both Alistair and Gabriel looked at her. Clara walked out into the hall, unable to have the conversation while she was trapped in Gabriel's gaze.

It was short and to the point. And she had some good news to give.

'We struck lucky. They managed to trace the hack right back to the offices of one of De-Marco Pharmaceuticals' biggest competitors. It was sloppy of them to do it from there, but they had a password for the system and the intrusion would have gone unnoticed once they'd logged off again.'

'Whose password?' Gabriel's face hardened. 'Mine?'

'No. Heidi Walker.'

Gabriel and Alistair stared at each other. Heidi's job as assistant to both of them meant that she had access to almost everything on the system.

'No. There must be some mistake.' Alistair was the first to speak.

'Unless… Heidi works from home sometimes. Maybe she had someone round to her place and he found her password…'

'*He?* What are you suggesting, Gabriel, that someone seduced our assistant and she told him her network password? I'd be surprised if even you could get away with slipping an enquiry about a woman's network password into a romantic conversation. And Heidi's a very sensible person, as you well know. It's all a little cloak and dagger, isn't it?'

Gabriel shrugged. 'I don't mean to imply that Heidi told anyone. She might have written it down somewhere.'

'Enough!' Gabriel and Alistair's way of starting at polar opposites to each other and working their way to a conclusion was effective but frustrating to watch, and Clara brought her hand down on the table with a little more force than she'd intended. 'Will you leave this to us? Our team will make discreet enquiries and see what they can find out. If and when they come up with something, I'll let you know.'

Gabriel nodded. 'All right. With one proviso, though. Heidi's worked with us for five years, and we presume her innocent unless there's irrefutable evidence to the contrary.'

'Yes,' Alistair agreed. 'We'd have to be one hundred per cent sure. One hundred and ten per cent. I don't believe that Heidi would do anything to hurt us.'

'No. Neither do I. She's clearly the victim in

this, and we must do everything we can to protect her.'

Clara took a deep breath. 'That goes without saying. No one's going to start accusing anyone unless there's solid proof, and there could well be a perfectly innocent explanation for this. Let's just concentrate on the good news, shall we? Knowing who's behind all of this is a major step forward.'

'Yes. Major step forward.' Alistair leaned back in his seat, yawning.

'It should never have happened in the first place.' Gabriel's face was dark. 'I always said I'd take a step back if the charity or any of our people were compromised. I think it's time I did that. I'm going to Italy in the morning, I'm a liability here.'

Alistair shook his head. 'You don't have to do that, Gabriel.'

'Yes. I do.' Gabriel had obviously made his mind up.

'Well… I suppose you could do with a break, after all that's happened. You'll love it there, Clara.'

'I'll be staying here, and I'll liaise with you, Alistair. There's a protection team from our Italian office in place at Gabriel's parents' home,' Clara interjected quickly.

Alistair turned the corners of his mouth down. 'Shame. You'll be missing a wonderful beach...'

'I'm not going for the beach, Alistair.' Gabriel seemed unable to sit still any longer, and got to his feet, opening the kitchen cupboard doors and then banging them closed again, as if he was looking for something.

'No, of course not. But you're never a liability.' Alistair finally said the words that Clara had been wanting to say.

'I'm not exactly an asset either. If Heidi or any of our staff have been compromised because of me, I won't forgive myself. I'll stay at my parents' place until this is all over.'

Which meant that he wouldn't need any more protection in England. He wouldn't need her any more. Clara felt as if she'd been punched in the stomach.

'If that's how you feel. I wish you'd stay but I can understand why you're going.' Alistair didn't seem to be putting up much of a fight to keep Gabriel here and Clara wanted to shake him.

'You'll cover for me while I'm gone?'

'Of course. I'll let Mike know you're out of the

country for a while, and keep an eye on him. We can set up a daily conference call to keep you up to speed.'

'Thanks. I think this is the best way to handle it.' Gabriel found what he was looking for, pulling a bottle of brandy from the back of one of the cupboards.

Alistair stretched his arms, yawning again. 'If you say so. We'll talk in the morning. I'm beat, I'd better call a taxi…'

'I'll get one of my team to take you home, Alistair. I've got to speak to my office to let them know what's going on, and arrange the car for the morning, so I'll be here until they get back.'

'Great. Thanks, I appreciate that.' Alistair got to his feet and reached for his jacket, following Clara out into the hallway. She needed to talk to Gabriel. If he was leaving tomorrow then she had to find some way of saying goodbye to him and keeping it professional, even if it did feel as if her heart was breaking.

'Is that a good idea?' When Clara walked back into the kitchen, Gabriel was splashing mixers into a glass.

'No. Probably not.' He took a sip of the concoction and wrinkled his nose. Clearly Gabriel's theory that not measuring ingredients made each drink unique was holding true. It looked as if this one was sour enough to match both their moods.

Clara took the glass from his hand, sniffing it and then throwing the contents into the sink. Gabriel watched her calmly.

'What's this? You're protecting me from myself now?'

'If you were thinking of staying up drinking, then you need to find a better excuse than telling yourself you're a liability to The Watchlight Trust.'

He shrugged. 'By tomorrow, I won't need to tell myself anything. I'll have my father to do it for me.'

Clara rolled her eyes. 'If he thinks you're such a liability, why does he want you to take over DeMarco Pharmaceuticals?'

'He thinks that DeMarco Pharmaceuticals is where I'm supposed to be. I'll be able to donate large chunks of cash to The Watchlight Trust, and that'll be a lot more use to them than I am. He might be right.'

'Stop it, Gabriel. The Watchlight Trust wouldn't even be there without you and Alistair, you created it. Taking a step back until this is all over might be a good idea, but it's a reaction to one specific situation. If you feel you really must drink and brood, then I'll be happy to mix the drinks for you, since you don't seem to be able to get them right tonight.'

'You'll drink and brood with me?'

Getting drunk with him on their last night together was tempting. So was Gabriel's sudden grin. But together those two ingredients had the potential for a whole world of mistakes.

'No. I said I'd mix the drinks, not drink them.'

'Ah. Not so enticing, then.' He picked up the bottle and stowed it back into the kitchen cupboard. 'I thought… I took it for granted that since I'm going to Italy for more than just a few days, you'd be coming with me.'

'The team there have local knowledge and they're much better placed to ensure your safety. It makes far more sense for me to stay here and work with Alistair.'

'I suppose you're right… Will you come with me anyway?'

Could things actually get any worse? Clara had just been forced into the realisation that she cared about Gabriel, and that it would be hard to leave him. Now he was suggesting that she pack her bags and follow him to Italy.

'Gabriel, you don't need me there. The team in Italy are excellent.'

'I'm sure they are, but you're the person I trust. If you feel able to come, of course...'

How many times did she have to tell him? It wasn't a matter of what *she* wanted. 'If you want me there, you should call the office.'

Gabriel shook his head. 'I'm not going to do that because...we've shared some moments of a personal nature. I won't pretend I wouldn't enjoy your company, but this is strictly a business trip. I don't want you to think it's anything else and I'm not going to be the one who tells you whether or not to come with me.'

It was an almost impossible choice. Staying here would be the safest thing, but she couldn't bear to leave Gabriel. Not now, when he'd been forced to abandon the thing that meant the most to him.

'Okay.' He seemed to know that she needed some time to think about this. 'Decide what you want to do and then call your office and tell them that it's at my specific request. I won't be leaving before half past ten tomorrow, so if you're coming make sure you get here by then. I'm going to bed now.'

He walked out of the kitchen. Clara stood, staring after him, long after he'd gone upstairs.

He trusted her. And he'd had the decency to let her know that he wasn't asking her to go to Italy with the aim of engineering a fleeting affair. Clara knew that he must feel the chemistry between them as keenly as she did, but he respected her professionalism and wanted her as a friend. She would do well to take a leaf out of Gabriel's book and treat him with the same kind of respect.

She sank down on one of the chairs at the kitchen table thinking hard, ignoring the fact that the night guard was probably downstairs watching all of this on the camera feed. At least it was a dumb show, and he hadn't heard what Gabriel had said.

She had to make a decision, one way or the other. Molly returned, popping her head around the kitchen door to let Clara know that she was back, after taking Alistair home. The team here at the house was back to full strength and Clara could leave now.

Tearing a sheet of paper from the pad in her

bag, she wrote a note for Gabriel, folding it in half and taping it to the coffee machine. Then she slipped out of the front door, and into the quiet night.

Don't go without me. I'm coming to Italy.

CHAPTER TWELVE

WHEN CLARA ARRIVED at the house at ten o'clock the following morning, Gabriel said nothing of their conversation the night before. But his sudden smile told her all she needed to know. Their bags were stowed in the boot of the SUV and they headed out of London to the small airfield where DeMarco Pharmaceuticals' private plane was waiting for them.

'What did Mr Sullivan say about your accompanying me?' A smile hovered around Gabriel's lips again.

'He said he thought you'd made a good decision.' Clara decided to leave it at that.

'Then we agree. I think it's a good decision, too.' Gabriel turned his head to look out of the car window, but even the back of his neck seemed to be smirking.

She'd travelled on a number of different aircraft, but this one had to be the most comfortable. Plenty of room, seats that could be adjusted to almost any position, and proper-sized tables to work and eat at. The stewardess offered them coffee when they boarded and an hour later a meal, which appeared to have been cooked from scratch in the small galley.

Two SUVs were waiting for them when they landed in Italy, and the team leader for Gladstone and Sullivan Securities Italian Division shook Clara's hand and promised her every co-operation. She felt positively rested and refreshed when they reached the beach house that was Leo and Alessia DeMarco's summer home.

Gabriel greeted his father with a handshake and his mother with a hug. Alessia DeMarco took Clara on a tour of the house, telling her that she must consider herself their guest, and Leo DeMarco remarked on how much he liked to hear English spoken with a London accent.

They were a charming, kindly couple, and Leo DeMarco not only looked like his son but his manner was much the same as Gabriel's too. Perhaps their similarities were why they didn't seem to get along so well. They gave every impression of being on the best of terms, but there was an underlying restraint and coolness between them.

Gabriel then took her to her room. Walking

outside, he climbed the steps up to a balcony at the back of the house, which overlooked the beach and the sea beyond. Leading her through a pair of French doors and into a comfortable upstairs sitting room, he explained that her bedroom was the door on the left, and his was the door on the right.

'Do you know where all the cameras are?' He looked around the room.

'I can't see any in here. I can find out.'

Gabriel nodded conspiratorially. 'Thanks.'

'So… Is there anything you'd like me to do?' The Italian team leader had made no bones about the fact that his team had everything under control.

'Not really. If you get bored…' He looked out of the window. 'I suppose with that view it's a little hard to get bored.'

'But if I *should* happen to?'

'Alistair's given me a few reports to look over while I'm here. I'd welcome your views at some point. If you get a moment…'

'My views. Not as a security systems specialist, I assume.'

'No, as a paramedic.' He had the grace to look a little sheepish. 'Lapsed paramedic.'

'Right. That'd be the job I gave up a while ago now.' The one that was so irrevocably tied to Tim's betrayal of her that it had been soured for ever.

'I understand if you don't feel able to do it.' His voice was suddenly tender.

Maybe Gabriel was right, and it was time to leave the betrayal behind. This was nothing to do with Tim, and the thought that Gabriel wanted her opinion prompted a little thrill of excitement.

'It's all right. I'll take a look.'

'Perfect. Thank you.' Gabriel turned on his heel and disappeared into his bedroom, only to reappear immediately with a thick, spiral-bound booklet. 'This is the one I'd really like you to look at. It's the first draft of our report on personal safety for rescue workers.'

'You had it ready?'

'I was just hoping you'd say yes.'

Clara rolled her eyes, and he grinned. Walking out onto the balcony and settling herself comfortably in the shade, she turned to the first page of the report and started to read.

The dream came again, because it always did on the first few nights he was back home. As if the closer he got to where Pietro had died, the easier it was for the cave to reach out and claw him back.

Gabriel sat up in bed, giving himself the same reminders he'd needed so many times before. Breathe. Wake up. Cold sweat ran down his spine and he shivered in the warmth of the night.

Then he realised. The connecting door between his bedroom and the sitting room stood open, and a dark shadow had detached itself from the others and was walking towards him. He wanted so much to hold Clara, and feel the living warmth of her body.

'Are you all right?'

'Yes. Sorry, bad dream. Did I wake you?'

'You cried out.' Clara sat down on the edge of the bed, far enough away from him that he couldn't reach her. Wise move.

'I…didn't realise…'

'I heard you muttering as well.'

Muttering. That generally involved words. Gabriel wondered if they'd been intelligible and, if so, what they were. No one had ever accused him of muttering in his sleep before.

But then no one had ever accused him of crying out in his sleep before either. The one thing about sex was that it always allowed him to sleep peacefully afterwards.

'Go back to bed, Clara. I'm sorry I disturbed you.'

'Isn't there something I can do?'

Not unless she wanted to stay and make him forget everything. She was wearing a pair of shorts and a vest top with thin straps over the shoulders, and the light that filtered through from the sitting room into his room was enough that he could make out the shape of her breasts.

'No. You really should go. I've been making a good job of keeping my promise.'

She gave a little nod of acknowledgement, her hair brushing her shoulders. Gabriel was sure he'd resisted greater temptations in his life, but couldn't remember quite when.

'That's not the only cure for night terrors.' Maybe she was going to let him hold her while he went back to sleep. It would be something new. He didn't remember a time when he'd just slept with a woman without making love to her.

'Put some clothes on. I'll be back in a moment.' Clara got to her feet, heading towards her own room.

He was wide awake now, and curious to see

what she had in mind. Hastily, he got out of bed, pulling on a pair of sweatpants and a T-shirt, and found her in the sitting room, wearing a zip-up top over her vest. Wordlessly, she took his hand, leading him downstairs and into the large kitchen.

'Sit…' She indicated a chair, and he sat down. Then she reached up to hook a small saucepan down from the rack, putting it onto the range and filling it with milk.

'A nightcap?' Gabriel grinned at her.

'Cocoa.' Clara had flipped open a few cupboards and found a packet, and she held it up for him to see. 'It's better for helping you sleep than sex any day of the week.'

'Whoever told you that isn't doing it properly.'

She chuckled, spooning the cocoa into the milk and stirring it as it heated. 'Well, maybe they're just so different that you can't really make a comparison.'

This was nice. None of the bustle and voices of the day. Just the two of them, with the sound of the sea crashing somewhere in the distance. She carried the mugs of cocoa to the table, sitting down opposite him.

'Thank you.'

'Do you want to talk about it?'

Gabriel had already shaken his head before it occurred to him that perhaps he *did* want to talk about it. Not speaking about the nightmares, keeping his own feelings to himself, had become second nature to him.

'It's…a long time ago. Done now. Finished.'

'Clearly *not* finished, for you. You were dreaming about what happened to your brother?'

Gabriel nodded, taking a sip of his cocoa.

'But you don't talk about it.' She was gentle, but Clara didn't seem to be about to give up. It occurred to Gabriel that he didn't want her to.

'My parents lost a son.'

'And you lost a brother. You had to fight to survive for three days.'

Guilt almost stopped his throat. 'I think that my survival was more a matter of chance. Most of the time I was just feeling sorry for myself.'

'So let me get this right.' She spoke quietly. 'You were eleven years old, and you'd seen your own brother and his friends buried in a rock fall. You had a broken ankle and no doubt a fair number of other minor injuries, and you were trapped underground in the darkness for three days…'

She broke off as Gabriel shivered violently. Reaching across the table, her fingertips touched his and he couldn't draw his hand away.

'I'm sorry, Gabriel, but I think you need to hear this. Just staying alive through all of that was an act of incredible bravery. Hasn't anyone told you that?'

'I don't talk about it all that much.'

'You mean never?'

Gabriel nodded. He wanted so much to tell her, but he didn't have the words. Maybe Clara could do what he couldn't, and find those words.

'Well, I'm not a doctor, specialising in the treatment of patients who've suffered trauma.' Her fingertips caressed his. 'I know a few things, though, and it's very obvious to me that you need to talk about this.'

His heart pounded in his chest. Three little words, that were so difficult to say, but which suddenly he couldn't hold back any more.

'Help me, Clara.'

They'd talked for a long time and it was clear that much of what Gabriel said was for the first time. It was hard to listen to, and hard to know how to respond. But he'd wanted to talk, and seemed to forgive Clara for not always knowing what to say in reply.

He didn't remember much about the last day he spent in the cave, or the first day after he was rescued. Maybe that was gone for good, like the night after he'd been dosed with flunitrazepam. It was clear that Gabriel needed a great deal more help with this than Clara could give him, but he seemed to be taking his first steps at least. As the sun rose, light slanting through the kitchen windows, they were still talking.

'After you were rescued, did your parents have you talk with anyone about your experiences?' He seemed to be feeding on her questions. Using them to help him to say the things he really needed to say.

'They took me to a number of different doctors. But I didn't talk. Full stop.'

'You mean…you didn't say anything?'

'Not a word. For five weeks.' Gabriel shrugged. 'My brother's funeral was delayed because of the time it took to dig the bodies out and perform the autopsies. I remember lying in bed the night before and hearing my father talking to my nanny. He said that my mother was beside herself with worry, and that they'd been talking about whether they should take me to the funeral. They couldn't decide what was best.'

He sighed, shaking his head.

'It was natural for them to be worried, Gabriel. That's not your fault.' He'd been very quick to blame himself for all of this.

'I was making things worse for her. She'd just lost Pietro… Anyway, the following morning I got out of bed while it was still dark. I dressed myself up in my best clothes and came downstairs, and found my parents right here, at this table. My mother was in her dressing gown, and she'd been crying…'

Clara caught her breath. This time she couldn't ask what had happened next, the picture of a young Gabriel dressing himself for his brother's funeral was too affecting.

'I told her that I wanted to go with them. I remember my mother bursting into tears and hugging me.'

'And…then?' Clara almost choked on the words.

'Then nothing. I went back to being a little boy. My sudden recovery was hailed as a miracle, my mother had her younger son back, although nothing could ever compensate for her having lost Pietro.'

'And you never spoke about it again?'

'It seemed… My mother took me back to all the doctors she'd taken me to before, but I told them that everything was okay. I wanted to be the kid who didn't worry his parents. They'd already been through enough.'

'You'd been through a lot too, Gabriel.' If he remembered nothing else of what she'd said tonight, Clara hoped he'd remember this. 'This is not something you can deal with on your own, you need professional help. You have to go and see someone and talk all of this through.'

He smiled suddenly. 'I've just told you, haven't I?'

'I'm not a counsellor. I can listen as a friend, and I'm glad you were able to tell me about this. But there's a difference between friendship and professional help, and I know you know that.'

'I'll think about it.' It didn't sound as if he was planning on doing any more than that.

'Seriously, Gabriel. I want you to think seriously about it. Because that's the advice you'd give to anyone else.'

He laughed suddenly, holding up his hands in a gesture of surrender. 'I'll think about it seriously. I promise.'

'And you'll go?'

'I didn't say that. But I will consider it very carefully.'

It was the most she was going to get out of him, and perhaps it was too much to ask for any more. Sitting up in the night, talking about it, was very different from committing himself to counselling. But he'd said he'd consider it so maybe Clara should count that as a win and forget about the losses.

'You're tired. You should go back to bed.'

That was a good suggestion. One she wasn't going to take up. Clara rose from her seat, stretching her limbs. 'I think I'll just get some coffee. I have things to do today.'

'Watching me?' He pursed his lips.

'Yes. Watching you.' Clara wasn't entirely sure how she was going to do that after the night they'd just shared. But that was the way of things with her and Gabriel. They shared so much in the quiet hours of the evening, and then went back to being strangers during the day.

'If I tell you that I'll stay put until you wake up, will you go to bed?' He grinned up at her. 'You can chain me to the kitchen table if you want, just to be sure.'

'Unfortunately, I don't carry chains. It's an oversight, I know.'

'Well, then, you can rip my head off if I take one step out of the house.'

'No can do, Gabriel. I'm supposed to be protecting you, and ripping your head off isn't covered in the contract.'

He got to his feet, walking round the table. Catching her hand in his, he brushed her fingers against his lips. 'I'll give you my word of honour, then. I won't leave the house until you wake up.'

Gabriel did it every time. That dark-eyed look that had her falling under his spell. And she was beginning to feel very tired. 'Okay. Not a step?'

'Not even a millimetre. Even if the place is on fire.'

Clara laughed sleepily. 'If the place is on fire you have my permission to leave. Not before you come and save me, though.'

'Understood. Consider yourself saved.'

He couldn't save her, though, could he? As Clara followed him upstairs, she couldn't help wishing that Gabriel could sweep her up in his arms and carry her away. Save her from wanting him, and knowing she couldn't have him.

But that wasn't going to happen. He was too

damaged. He'd tried so hard to be the son that his parents wanted, and in doing so he'd shut himself away. Maybe one day he'd learn that love wasn't solely a matter of duty, but by then she'd be long gone.

He walked through the sitting room and opened her bedroom door, staying on the threshold. 'Get into bed.'

'Okay…okay.' She tried to pull the bedcovers straight and gave it up as a bad job. Asking him to come and tuck her in wasn't going to work well…

Clara climbed into the bed, unzipping her sweatshirt and wriggling out of it. It dropped onto the floor, but she couldn't be bothered to get up again and pick it up.

'Close your eyes.'

'Are you still here?' She was half-asleep already.

Gabriel chuckled, and she heard the door close quietly.

CHAPTER THIRTEEN

IT WAS GOOD to see Clara lose her guardedness. It was one thing for Gabriel to feel that he was looking over his shoulder—that was a relatively recent development in his life. But it seemed wrong that she should be doing it for a living. She had so much else to give.

It was her decision. But asking her to do what she really was best at seemed reasonable enough. She'd seemed to enjoy commenting on the draft report, and she'd made a very thorough job of it. So Gabriel gave Clara another couple of reports to read through.

The sea breeze and the sun kissed her cheeks, where he couldn't. Wearing something that blended in became a matter of summer dresses, and shorts and T-shirts for hikes along the beach. His parents both liked her, and he saw his father showing her around the walled garden at the side of the house, which was his pride and joy, delicate plants protected from the wind by high brick walls.

'Nice flower.' When Clara joined him on the balcony outside his private sitting room, Gabriel nodded towards the bright bloom that she'd pinned to the front of her dress. 'That's quite a compliment, you know. My father doesn't give flowers to just anyone.'

Clara smiled. 'He's very kind. And he knows so much about all the different plants. He's even got some that are medicinal.'

'Well, that's the best of both worlds for him. He likes plants and he's got an interest in medicines as well.' Gabriel stared out at the tranquil sea.

'All that digging must be hard work. He's not getting any younger.' Clara dropped the remark so casually that anyone would think it had no point to it. But Gabriel knew that it probably did. Clara seldom said anything without weighing it up first.

'He's never asked me.'

'Funny. That's the same thing he says about you.'

Gabriel puffed out a breath. He loved it that Clara wanted to help, but there was no changing his relationship with his father. Not even Clara could work that kind of magic.

'My father and I…we co-exist. He's a part of my life and I'm a part of his, but if we spend any appreciable length of time together we end up arguing.'

'He talks about you, though. He was telling me about teaching you to swim when you were little. Teaching you and your cousin how to climb…'

The thought of those days made Gabriel's heart ache. He'd had a great childhood, and he owed that to a man he hardly even spoke to now.

'It's hard to explain, Clara. Things were a lot simpler when I was a kid, my parents were a bit over-protective but I understood why. They just wanted me to be all right, and it was easy enough to fulfil that ambition for them.'

'And now?'

'Now? He wants to retire, but he needs to find someone to continue in his place. He's handing everything that he's worked so hard to build over to me. What kind of son and heir would I be if I refused to take it on?'

Clara frowned, and Gabriel reached out, brushing the back of her hand with his fingers. 'I appreciate that you care, Clara. My father and I get on best when we don't spend too much time alone together. We know how to play nice with each other when we're with family or in the boardroom.'

'Have you never told him that you'd prefer to keep working with the charity *you've* built? That you don't want to take over DeMarco Pharmaceuticals?'

'No. It's my duty to take over from him. I'm the only son he has left.' That was fixed, and there was no way to escape it. But it hadn't happened yet… Gabriel rose from his seat, looking out at the sea. 'Would you like to come swimming?'

'Forget about tomorrow and live for today, you mean?' Clara always seemed able to read his thoughts.

'Yeah. I've got a video conference with Alistair and then the Dream Team in an hour, and I could do with a bit of exercise first to clear my head.'

Clara nodded, taking the flower from her dress and dropping it into the half-drunk glass of water by Gabriel's chair. 'Okay. A swim sounds nice. I'll race you down there…'

That evening the four of them had gathered around the huge kitchen table as usual for dinner. Clara had worn the flower on her dress and received a smiling compliment from his father, which was much the same as the one that Gabriel would have given her if he'd felt able to.

His mother was smiling, and they lingered over dessert and coffee. Clara was becoming the glue that held them together. Almost as if this was a proper family again, instead of a broken one.

As the days went by, Gabriel began to see the strain that his father had been under. There had been questions about DeMarco Pharmaceuticals' ability to properly test the new drug, which had to be answered in detail. His father had been called away for the day to attend a press tour of their new manufacturing plant, to deflect allegations that the conditions for their workers were below standard, and arrived home looking more world-weary than Gabriel had ever seen him.

He was at a loss. He knew he should have been there for his father, but his attempts at support were dismissed. When his father raged, it was Clara who calmed him, with her businesslike daily report of the security situation, which gave practical ways in which each issue was being handled. If there had ever been any doubt about the value of bringing her here, it was dispelled.

Gabriel could rest easy that his own personal reasons could stay well hidden.

They'd been in Italy for a week when she called the family to the kitchen table, making sure that everyone was sitting down and had coffee before she spoke. It was either a very bad sign or a very good sign, and Gabriel wondered which.

'I'm happy to tell you that we have solid evidence against the people responsible for the attacks on your family.' There was real warmth in her sudden smile. 'Because these attacks involved computer hacking, an attempt to do Gabriel physical harm by drugging him and various other criminal activities, it's now a police matter.'

His mother clapped her hands together, smiling. All she needed to know was that the family was safe. Gabriel needed to know more.

'Heidi… Has she been exonerated?'

Clara nodded. 'Yes, completely. There was someone else at the charity's offices who's currently being interviewed by the police.'

'Who?' Gabriel felt the hairs on the back of his neck stand up. He couldn't think of anyone that he didn't trust.

'Philip Atkinson.'

His mother and father looked at Gabriel questioningly and he shrugged. 'Philip's our work experience student. He's only seventeen, I interviewed him myself when he took him on. Are you sure about this, Clara?'

'We're sure. And actually he's twenty-four. But I've seen the photographs, and I agree with you that he looks seventeen. He stole Heidi's diary out of her bag, after seeing her look up her new network password. She'd written it down because we gave everyone secure passwords and no one could remember them.'

'How did you find out?'

'We did a preliminary check on all of the staff's CVs. Philip's date of birth was flagged up immediately as being wrong, so we investigated a little further. He was confronted with the evidence against him, and he gave up the person responsible. It turns out that the whole campaign was masterminded by a rather ambitious junior executive working for the company that we traced the computer hack back to. It appears that he was acting alone, in the belief that securing the manufacturing rights for your new drug would fast-track him straight onto the board of directors of his own company. They're furious with him and have washed their hands of the whole business.'

'I doubt they'd be complaining too much if the manufacturing rights had just fallen into their laps.' Gabriel turned the corners of his mouth down.

'No, I doubt that too. But it's pretty clear they didn't know anything about the attacks, and they've been very anxious to help in determining if any of their other staff were involved.'

'Why Gabriel?' His mother spoke suddenly and Gabriel could see tears forming in her eyes. 'Why target my son?'

Clara took a moment to think, understanding how important this was to his mother. 'Because you love him enough to ask that question. Your care kept him safe, too.'

Alessia nodded, dabbing her eyes.

'Thank you, Clara. You're a marvel.' Gabriel's father spoke. It was good to see both his parents reassured and smiling, and Gabriel offered his own silent thanks to Clara.

'You're very kind, but it wasn't actually my doing. You have our investigative team to thank for this. They've worked very hard.'

'So…what now?' Gabriel felt a lump forming

in his throat. This was nothing but good news, apart from the fact that Clara's help would clearly no longer be needed.

'We still proceed with caution. But the police have found paperwork on all the attacks, along with some that were planned for the future, and are confident that they have everyone that was involved. This is definitely the end of this campaign.'

'And you? Will you be going back to London?' Suddenly Gabriel's gaze met hers. For a moment he saw all of the warmth that he'd only ever seen before when they were alone. Then she looked down at the tabletop.

'Mr Sullivan says that if the family agrees, the protection teams here and in London can now be safely withdrawn. So I'll be leaving in the morning...'

He thought he heard Clara stumble a little over the words. But she wouldn't look at him and he couldn't gauge what she was thinking.

'No...' The only thing he knew was that he couldn't let Clara go now.

'I think what Gabriel means...' his mother came to his rescue '...is that we are poor hosts at the moment. But if you would like some time to relax and enjoy the beach, we would be very pleased to have you here with us. Maybe you could fly back to London with Gabriel on Friday, rather than rushing back tomorrow?'

His mother had voiced the words in his heart. Tomorrow was the anniversary of Pietro's death and Clara would inevitably be left to her own devices. But all the same, he wanted her to stay. Maybe they'd have a chance to talk a little, free of the iron restrictions that professionalism had put onto their relationship.

'That's a fine idea, Alessia.' His father seemed to approve too. 'A few days' relaxation, without having to keep up with Gabriel's antics.'

Gabriel swallowed down the impulse to tell his father that he hardly thought his actions fell under the category of *antics.* Petty disagreements didn't matter now, all that mattered was that the burden had been lifted from his parents. And that he wanted very much for Clara to stay.

'My mother's right. Spend a few days winding down and come back to London with me.' It was a simple enough proposal, but he was suddenly as nervous as a teenager.

'If that's all right with everyone?' She hesitated, looking at him questioningly, and Gabriel resisted the urge to ask her whether she'd been listening. Instead he gave her a nod.

'Then I'd love to stay, thank you. I don't have to be back at work until next Monday so flying back on Friday would be ideal.'

'Then that's settled.' Gabriel's mother gave the broad smile that he should have offered and stood, walking over to the range. 'Tonight I think I will cook something special.'

The anniversary of Pietro's death dawned bright and clear, the sun glinting across a dark blue sea. When Clara went downstairs for breakfast she found Gabriel alone at the kitchen table.

'Where are your parents?'

'Walking.' Gabriel gestured towards the open patio doors, and she saw his mother and father, walking together along the beach. 'They always do the same thing. Walk a bit in the morning, and then have lunch. In the afternoon, my mother will go to the cave and leave some flowers. My father doesn't go, she goes with the mothers of the other four boys.'

'Is it safe for them to go there?'

'Yes, it's safe. My father talked to the other families, and they decided that they wanted to open the cave up again. It's really very beautiful, and they all felt that they wanted to have somewhere to go where they could remember their sons. So my father had it made safe and walkways put in. Lights…'

'But you've never been.'

He looked up at her from his coffee. 'No. I've never been.'

Clara poured herself some coffee and collected a pastry from the large plate on the counter, joining Gabriel at the table. 'What are you going to do today?'

He hesitated. 'I hadn't thought about it. I'm sorry, I should be a better host…'

'That's not important. Take some time to do whatever *you* want to do. I'll be here if you want some company.'

'Thanks but…' He seemed about to say something and then thought better of it. He got up from the table and refilled his coffee cup. 'If you don't mind, I've got some work to do. It's just routine paperwork but I'd better get started.'

Routine paperwork. By definition that could have waited until another day, but Gabriel seemed intent on doing it now. Clara looked out across the beach to where his parents were walking, his mother's dress blowing in the wind and flapping against his father's legs. They seemed so united in their grief, but Gabriel seemed determined to be alone in his.

The house had been silent all day. Clara had taken a short walk and then retreated to her room to read the papers that Gabriel had given her, and write her report. If she couldn't help, then the least she could do was keep out of the way. She left her bedroom door open, an invitation for him to come in if he wanted, but he stayed away.

At four o'clock she stretched her back and arms, and walked out onto the balcony. The sea breeze tugged at her hair, blowing at the cobwebs of the day, which stubbornly refused to dissipate. She could see the beach path and…

Running along the path, three small figures. The urgency in their movements made Clara lean forward, straining her eyes to see who they were. Gabriel's mother and two other women. Something wasn't right.

Clara turned, running down the steps from the balcony and making her way towards the path. Leo must have seen them too, because he was running from the walled garden towards his wife. They met at the top of the path.

'Leo...' Alessia stopped for a moment to get her breath. 'Matilde and Giulia are still in the cave... Matilde wanted to go back, and Giulia went with her.'

This seemed to be a matter of some concern. Leo's brow darkened. 'Are you sure?'

One of the other woman spoke in Italian, and Alessia nodded. 'Yes, we're sure. They went and they haven't returned.'

'Can't we go and see whether they're all right?' Clara turned to Leo, wondering why that hadn't been done already.

'The tide is in. No one can get in or out of the cave.'

'How long for?'

'All night.' Alessia was in tears now. 'Something must have happened...'

This wasn't good. Even if both of them were all right, they couldn't stay there all night, trapped in the place where their sons had died. On the anniversary of their deaths.

'Is there any way we can get there? Can we go by boat?'

Leo shook his head. 'That would be madness,

no one can take a boat through those rocks. There's the borehole, though, the one we sank to get into the cave. It hasn't been used for many years, but it may be a way in.'

Alessia pressed her lips together. She clearly didn't want to ask anyone to go that route, but she was desperately worried for her friends.

'Where is it? I'll go and find Gabriel—'

'No!' His father laid his hand on her arm. 'He cannot be there, Clara. We cannot ask him to help.'

They had to. Not just for practical reasons but for Gabriel's sake.

'You must give him the chance. If you make this choice for him now, he may never forgive you for it.'

Leo hesitated, glancing at Alessia, who nodded.

'Very well. Ask the gardener to find some torches, they'll be in the garage somewhere. Tell Gabriel what's happened and let him make his decision. We'll meet you where the path runs along the top of the cliff.'

It can't have been easy for him, but Leo had done the right thing. As he began to usher the women back down the path, Clara turned and ran for the house.

* * *

He'd thought that he'd made it clear he wanted to be alone. But when Clara burst into his room, breathless from running, Gabriel knew that something was wrong.

'What is it?'

'Two of the women your mother was with this afternoon went back to the cave and the tide's in now and they're trapped. Your father and mother have gone to the borehole to see if there's a way in through there.'

Cold fear curled in his stomach. 'They think it'll be possible to get in that way?'

'I don't know. Your father says it's the only chance and he asked me to tell you—'

'Tell me what? To stay here?' His own voice seemed to be coming from somewhere far away, and it had bitterness in it.

'To make your own decision, Gabriel. I'm going back now to help them, the gardener's fetching me some torches from the garage and I need the first-aid kit as well. If I can make it into the cave through the borehole…'

Somehow his heart found the courage to propel him to his feet. 'I'll get the first-aid kit, it's in the kitchen. You might like to get changed.'

She met him in the kitchen, no longer wearing her summer dress but a pair of jeans with a sweatshirt and trainers. Together they hurried to the garage, where the elderly gardener was waiting with the torches. Gabriel hunted amongst the boxes at the back, and found what he was looking for.

'What's in there?' Clara picked up the torches and the first-aid kit as he slung the large, zipped bag over his shoulder.

'It's my cousin's climbing equipment.'

'How long has it been in storage here?' Clara frowned at him as they hurried from the garage, towards the cliff path.

'Only since last month. My father taught us both to climb when we were teenagers and he still comes down here a couple of times every summer to take on the cliffs further down the coast. He's very careful about his equipment so the ropes will be fine.'

Clara gave him a tight smile. 'That's my way down, then.'

'*Your* way down?' His mouth was suddenly dry. Gabriel knew what he had to do, there was no decision to be made. But that didn't mean he had to like it.

'Well, your mother and father aren't going down there, that's for sure.'

'I know how to climb, and I'm a doctor. I'm the obvious choice…' He tried to sound nonchalant about it and failed miserably.

She didn't slacken her pace, but he felt Clara's hand on his arm. 'No one can ask that of you, Gabriel. It's too much.'

'Clara, don't make me argue with you, because I can't say this more than once. If you're set on going down there, that's up to you, but I'm coming with you.'

'Can't keep you away, can I?' She pursed her lips, looking up at him. 'Your parents are going to kill me. But, okay, if you feel you can do it when we get there, we'll go together.'

The borehole was situated some way back from the cliff path, in a dip in the ground. A low stone wall encircled it, and Gabriel could see his father fumbling with the combination of the last padlock, which secured a heavy metal grille across the top. His mother and her friend were watching, holding each other's hands.

His father tried to heave the grille open but it was too heavy for him. Gabriel hurried down the incline, dumping the bag and taking hold of the other side of the grille.

'Let me help you.'

His father nodded, and slowly they lifted the grille open, the heavy hinges groaning as they did so. Clara shone a torch downwards and Gabriel could see that bands of solid rock ran around the sides of the borehole. He hadn't realised how much effort it must have taken for his own rescuers to drill down into the cave.

He wasn't going to think about that. He needed to focus on now, today, and the women who were down there and needed his help.

'There's a ladder.' Clara shone the beam of the torch onto the metal ladder that was fixed to the side of the borehole.

'Yeah. Who knows how stable it is, after all this time.' It looked sturdy enough to Gabriel, but if it wasn't it was a thirty-foot drop.

She bent down, opening the bag, pulling out a harness and a coil of nylon rope, sorting through the other equipment. 'There are a couple of belay devices here. I think it's going to be safer just to abseil down there. I'll go first.'

Gabriel nodded. 'Okay. Wait for me when you get to the bottom.'

His mother and father watched, silent and tight-lipped as Clara put on the harness and adjusted it, while Gabriel secured the rope around the heavy metal brackets that locked the grille in place. Then he took a harness from the bag, putting it on, and Clara checked it for him and fixed two belay devices to the rope, working quietly and carefully to make sure he'd missed nothing.

'You've got this?' She murmured the words quietly.

'Yes. Let's get on with it.'

Clara turned to his mother, taking her hand. 'I've done this lots of times before, and I've checked everything to make sure it's safe. We're going to find your friends, and we'll be back in no time. Try not to worry.'

His mother nodded and Gabriel felt a lump in his throat. As he watched Clara step over the side of the parapet he felt physically sick. She gave him a broad grin and started to abseil down the borehole, the light of her torch bouncing this way and that as she went.

He felt his father's hand on his arm. 'I will go in your place…'

'No. I won't let Clara go alone, and I need to

do this.' Gabriel wondered if his father could understand. He'd never done so before.

'I know. You are a doctor.' His father nodded.

'Yes, I am. And I need you here, to call for help if we need it.'

'You don't remember when we brought you out of here, do you?'

'No.'

His father smiled suddenly. 'I lifted you out in my arms. I'll be waiting here for you today, too.' His father reached for him, enveloping him in a hug.

'Hey! What's going on up there?' Clara's voice echoed upwards and Gabriel broke free of his father. Suddenly he knew that he could do this.

'What's going on down there?' he called down to her.

'I'm in a smallish cave, it looks as if it leads through to the larger one. Shall I go and see if I can find them?'

'No, wait for me.' Gabriel swung his legs over the parapet. As he slid slowly down the rope, he saw the circle of sky above his head diminish. He felt his feet hit the floor of the borehole, and just as panic began to tear at the pit of his stomach he felt Clara take hold of his arm.

She unclipped his harness from the rope. ‘Are you good to go?’

‘Yes. Let’s find them.’ Gabriel took her hand, leading the way.

CHAPTER FOURTEEN

CLARA WAS BEGINNING to wonder whether she'd done the right thing. It was clear that Gabriel was hanging on by a thread. But he needed this chance to prove himself, and if one or both of the women was injured then she was going to need him.

Lights glimmered up ahead of them, and as they stepped into the larger cave he seemed to steady. More space, and more light, and by the gleam of the lights fixed to the wall, which marked out a smooth and easy walkway through the cave, she could see two figures on the far side. One rose, and hurled its way across the cave towards them.

The woman flung her arms around Gabriel's waist, hugging him tight. 'Gabriel… Gabriel.'

'Giulia.' Gabriel held her, soothing her. She started to speak to him, quick and urgent words in Italian that Clara couldn't follow. Gabriel was listening intently, walking her over to where the other woman lay, a folded coat under her head.

'She says that Matilde became very drowsy and suddenly just sat down. Then she flopped over onto her side…' He spoke to Giulia again, questioning her. 'She doesn't know if Matilde has any medical conditions, she's a proud woman and probably wouldn't say if she had.'

It could be any number of things. Clara bent down beside Matilde, examining her carefully while Gabriel questioned Giulia again. In the dim light Matilde looked very pale and she was muttering, quietly but incoherently.

Clara checked Matilde's wrists and throat, and found what she was looking for. A disc, bearing a symbol she knew well on a chain around her neck.

'Gabriel. What does this say?' She unfastened the chain, holding the medical alert disc out.

Gabriel turned it over in his hand, still comforting a weeping Giulia. 'She has Type 2 diabetes. You're thinking hypoglycaemia?'

Clara bent over Matilde again, smelling her breath and laying her hand on her forehead. 'All her symptoms are in line with hypoglycaemia. Don't suppose you have any sweets in your pocket, do you?'

'Afraid not.' He turned to Giulia, speaking quickly to her, and she shook her head. Apparently she didn't have much of a sweet tooth either.

'There's nothing in Matilde's bag…'

'We need to try to get something sweet into her before she loses consciousness completely. You go and see if my father can send something down. I'll stay here with her.'

Clara hesitated. Could she leave Gabriel here alone with the women? Might he suddenly begin to panic? But if she stayed, she wouldn't understand what either of the women were saying to her.

'It's okay. Go.' He murmured the words without looking at her, but they were enough. Clara hurried back to the bottom of the borehole, seeing Leo's face appear in the circle of sunlight above her head.

'We need a sugary drink. Can you get something from the house? Matilde's diabetic…'

'Sì, sì…' Leo had lapsed into Italian, and there seemed to be other people at the top of the borehole now. Probably staff from the house, who'd

been alerted to what was happening by the gardener.

There seemed to be some conversation going on, and Clara shifted impatiently. She needed some action. 'Leo, we need to hurry…'

Gabriel's father leaned over the parapet, looking down at her. 'Someone's going now. We have Matilde's bag here, she left it with Alessia. Might she have brought something?'

Another bag. Of course. Clara should have thought that if Matilde was travelling here today she wouldn't just have brought her handbag. 'Send it down, Leo. We can find what we need.'

There was a pause and another rope, with a nylon shopping bag attached to it, came spinning down the shaft. Clara grabbed at it, looking through the contents. When she unzipped one of the side pockets she found a make-up bag, and inside was an injection kit and some sachets of what might be glucose, the printing on the outside in Italian.

'I think that's what we need. Send the drink down when you get it, just in case.' Leo and Alessia must be sick with worry. 'I'm going back to Gabriel now. Everything's going to be okay.'

'Thank you. Go…'

Clara ran back to the main cave, opening the make-up bag and taking out the contents. 'Is this what we need?' She handed him one of the sachets and he glanced quickly at the writing on the packet.

'Where did you get this?'

'Matilde brought another bag, she'd left it with your mother.' Clara reached for the first-aid kit, opening it and finding some hand wipes. 'It's glucose?'

'Yes. Let's see if we can get her sitting up.' He took the hand wipe, cleaning his fingers quickly and slipping on a surgical glove from the box. Together he and Clara sat Matilde up, Gabriel supporting her with one arm around her back, and she muttered something.

Clara tore the packet of glucose open, and Gabriel dipped his finger into it. More talk, and Matilde opened her mouth a little way, letting him dab a little bit of the glucose onto her tongue. Then her head lolled to one side.

'Matilde!' Gabriel rapped out what sounded like an order in Italian. She opened her eyes and stuck out her tongue, and Gabriel fed her another small dab of glucose.

Giulia was still crying softly behind them, and

Matilde muttered something in Italian. Gabriel grinned, turning to say something to Giulia, and she nodded, stepping back to sit on a smooth outcrop of rock, wiping her face with her sleeve.

'She told Giulia to stop making such a fuss. I said that she must be feeling better.' Gabriel was still feeding Matilde the glucose bit by bit so that she didn't choke.

'When she wakes up a bit more, she'll be glad we did.'

Gabriel quirked the corners of his mouth down. 'Yeah. However much she might want to stay here, she has some more things to do. On the outside…'

Was that how he felt? That he'd wanted to stay here, with his brother? Clara supposed he must have done and that maybe he was saying something of the sort to Matilde. Gabriel was talking to her quietly, and whatever he was saying seemed to comfort her.

'Go and see if my dad's sent the drink down yet.' *My dad.* Clara had been aware that Gabriel and his father had been talking as she'd abseiled down the shaft, and wondered what they'd said. She'd never heard him refer to his father as *dad.*

Maybe it had been a slip of the tongue. There

would be time to talk about it later. Clara hurried to the bottom of the shaft, finding a bag with a bottle of orange juice and a plastic cup inside lying at her feet.

'Thanks. She's starting to come out of it now. Gabriel's okay too,' she called up to Leo, who nodded in reply, passing the news on in Italian.

'The mountain rescue team will be half an hour.'

'That's great. I don't think that either she or Giulia will be able to get up with what we have here. I'm going back now, but I'll let you know if anything happens.'

'*Grazie*, Clara.' Alessia leaned over the parapet, smiling down at her. Clara knew that Alessia wanted to hug Gabriel, and she'd be able to do so soon enough. In the meantime, she would take the best care of him.

By the time the mountain rescue team arrived, Matilde was sitting up, leaning against Gabriel and talking. The make-up bag had contained a blood-testing kit, and Gabriel had administered the thumb prick and declared Matilde's blood sugar level to be nearing acceptable.

He lifted her up, talking to the young woman

paramedic who had abseiled down with the climbers as they carried Matilde to the bottom of the shaft. Matilde was fixed securely into the chair hoist, and one of the team climbed with her to the top. The chair was lowered again, and Giulia kissed Gabriel on both cheeks, before stepping forward to be hoisted to the top of the shaft.

'They'll take good care of her.' Gabriel stood, looking up at the circle of light above them, gesturing towards the climbing ropes. 'Ladies first…'

'I'm not leaving you down here alone. You go. Wait for me at the top.'

He didn't move. Slipping his hands in his pockets, Gabriel looked upwards, and then back over his shoulder towards the main cave.

'Would you like to go back for a minute? I'll come with you, if you want.' Clara didn't know what she'd do or say if Gabriel wanted to go alone. Maybe she should let him, but she doubted whether her legs would take her to the top of the shaft while he was still here.

'Yes, I'd like that. Thank you.' He turned his face up to the top of the shaft, where his father was leaning over the parapet, looking down, and called up to him. 'Give me ten minutes, Dad. Everything's okay...'

His father nodded, holding out his arm and tapping the face of his watch. 'Ten minutes, son.'

No arguments, and no explanations. Gabriel's father seemed to know what he wanted, and was going to let him do it. Just as long as it didn't take any more than ten minutes.

Stick to the schedule. Gabriel flashed a smile as he mouthed the words to Clara, and then he turned, walking back towards the main cave. She followed him standing to one side as he walked over to the place where Matilde and Giulia had been, sitting down on the bench.

Opposite him, the flowers that the women had brought were together in one large vase. Above it, Clara could see a small motif carved into the rock. Five abstract figures, the lines seeming to be leaping together towards the sun. The five boys who'd died here.

Gabriel was staring at it, lost in thought. Maybe she should go back to the outer cave and leave him to do whatever he needed, but he turned, holding his hand out to her. She sat down next to him on the bench and he put his arm around her shoulder. When she leaned against him, she could feel that he was trembling, his heart beating fast.

'The families wanted something…a little different. Something about life, not death.' He nodded towards the carved figures.

'It's perfect, Gabriel.'

His chest heaved as he took a deep breath. As if he wanted to remind himself that he was alive and his lungs still needed air.

'This place… It's beautiful. And terrible as well.'

It *was* beautiful. Mineral deposits and crystals caught the light, and the rocks were streaked with colour. Different layers, pressed together over thousands of years, to produce a little piece of nature's artistry. Suddenly, Gabriel got to his feet, catching her hand and leading her over to a dark corner of the cave. He bent down, his fingers searching for something, and Clara heard the quiet splash of water.

'You knew this was here?' A tiny underground stream, which appeared from the rock for little more than a metre then disappeared again.

'I found it.' He reached out, dangling his fingers in the water, and Clara knelt down beside him. The water was cold, and must have brought a little hope to the boy who had found it. When her fingers touched his, he smiled.

He cupped his hand, raising it to his lips and taking a sip. Wrinkling his nose, he turned away, spitting the water out. 'It doesn't taste as good as I remember it.'

'If it's all you have…' Clara decided not to issue a reminder that drinking from streams wasn't a good idea. He'd survived it once.

'Yeah.' He got to his feet, holding out his hand to help her up. Then he wrapped his arms around her shoulders.

It was all the warmth, all the electricity of having Gabriel close. But it was more than that, too. Another heart beating against hers, reminding them both that they were alive. That they could walk away from here and feel the sun on their faces.

'You know…every time I think I'm getting to really know you, you go and surprise me again.'

Clara smiled up at him. 'What did I do this time? The abseiling?'

'No. Although I have to admit that it's got me wondering how I could ever bear the company of a woman who can't abseil.'

'Enough of the charm, Gabriel.' Clara nudged him, and he chuckled.

'All right. What really struck me is that medicine seems to be the one thing that really fulfils you.'

Clara shrugged. 'I just have enough medical knowledge to be of some help. There's nothing wrong with helping people, is there?'

'No, of course not. But you were on a mission this afternoon, you weren't going to give up until you'd found Matilde and Giulia. And even though it was serious business, there was a kind of light about you…'

A lump began to form in Clara's throat. However much she tried to deny it, he was right. 'I suppose…old habits die hard.'

'Or—you could just say that you were born to do this. That making a difference matters to you, and that medicine is where you make your difference.'

Clara laid her hand on his chest, feeling tears prick at the sides of her eyes. The truth hurt. 'Don't, Gabriel. You know why I left medicine and…please don't do this. We did something good this afternoon, that's all I want to hear from you.'

He nodded, his face tender. 'As you wish. You did something very good, Clara.'

'You too, Gabriel.'

He nodded a thank-you. But however much Clara tried to convince herself that she didn't want to talk about it, she knew what Gabriel thought. And maybe she thought the same. Maybe giving up medicine had been one of the biggest mistakes she'd ever made.

But she'd made it and the only way was forward. And Gabriel seemed to have reached his own limit now. She felt his body tremble against hers. However much he'd needed to come back here, he also needed to tear himself away.

'Is it time to go?' She reached up, her fingers aching to caress his face. Instead, she brushed them against the collar of his shirt.

'Yeah, I think so.' He turned, taking her hand, and they walked together out of the cave.

Something had changed. Something so enormous that Gabriel couldn't work out quite how he felt about it. He just felt. Anger and love, guilt and release. Too many things to put a name to them.

His father seemed distant again. He'd helped

both him and Clara up out of the borehole, telling them they'd done a good job, and then turned away from Gabriel. As if the emotion he'd shown had been a mistake.

Matilde's daughter had arrived, and the young woman paramedic had driven them both away, bearing everyone's hugs and good wishes. Everyone else had trooped back to the house, and gone to sit on the veranda, to drink tea and watch the sea. His mother and Giulia and their two other friends talked amongst themselves, and Clara sat between Gabriel and his father. She was working hard to keep the conversation going between them, and failing. Gabriel wondered if this afternoon had just been all a dream. He wanted to be alone suddenly, and rose from his seat, walking down towards the sea.

'Do you want to know what I think?' It seemed that he'd been staring out at the horizon for a long time when Clara's voice pulled him back again.

'Always.'

'I think you should talk to your father.'

Gabriel shook his head. 'You think one afternoon can change everything?'

'No. But if you want to change things, there's always a point at which you start.'

It was too complicated. There had been too many years of trying to be someone that he wasn't, and he couldn't see a way forward now. Gabriel was pretty sure that the sea couldn't tell him the answer but he kept looking anyway. Somehow it calmed him.

'Gabriel… Gabriel, listen to me.' She took his arm, and Gabriel realised that this was the first time she'd ventured this much. They never touched when there was a possibility that anyone else could see, and they were standing in full view of the house.

'I always listen to you, Clara.'

'Your father made a mistake. You were eleven years old and you didn't want to talk. He was the adult and he should have found some way to reach you, but I can see why he didn't. He had his own grief to deal with.'

That was a very fair synopsis. Apart from one thing. 'It's not all his fault. I'm not eleven any more and I've never reached out to him.

'And you had your reasons for that. Grief, trauma. The idea that a parent always knows best, however old we get.'

'That lets me off the hook, then. Just for the record, I'm not entirely comfortable with that. I should carry more of the blame…' He tried to make a joke of it.

'He's a good man, Gabriel, and he loves you.'

'I know. I love him, too.'

'If you love him then you have to talk to him. He's lost one son already, don't make him lose another by allowing the company to drive a wedge between you.'

Clara always made him feel as if he could do anything. As if the world contained no walls, no hidden underground chambers where he was afraid to go. Gabriel turned his face up to the sun, but it didn't warm him as much as the woman standing by his side.

'Will you do one thing for me?'

'Depends what it is.' She smiled up at him.

'Take a walk along the beach first. Maybe we can watch the sunset.' He smiled back at her. 'In an entirely platonic fashion, of course. We could appreciate the scientific reasons for sunsets and red skies…'

She chuckled. 'We could if I had any idea what they were.'

'You don't?' Gabriel pulled a face of mock

horror. 'Well, there isn't a jot of romance in any of it. Just hard science…'

His definition of hard science was to escort her to one of the flat rocks on the beach and bid her to stand quite still on it.

'You—as the sun—are both brilliant and have an irresistible gravitational pull. Whereas I—as a minor third planet—can only revolve around you. Spinning helplessly…'

Right. And this had nothing to do with romance. In that case, hard science was unexpectedly thrilling.

'When my back's to you, it's cold and dark. When I face you, I'm blinded…' He shaded his eyes and Clara laughed.

'Okay, I'm overawed with your demonstration, even though I already knew that bit. What's it got to do with a red sunset?'

He grinned. 'Because different parts of the spectrum are scattered in different ways by the earth's atmosphere. When you're straight in front of me I see more blues and yellows. Hence a blue sky.'

'And when you turn away?' Gabriel *would* turn away from her, and now that she was no longer working with him it would be happening sooner than she'd thought. They were two very different people, who could take some time together but not for ever.

'When I turn away…' he twisted sideways '… my last glimpse of you is full of the regret of knowing you're almost gone…'

'I'll take it as read that you're experiencing a world of regret. Why is the sky red?'

'Because the angle means that the light's taking a longer path through the earth's atmosphere. More of the blue and yellow parts of the spectrum are removed, leaving the red.'

Clara removed her shoes, climbing down from the rock to stand with him in the gently rolling surf. These few days were never going to happen again. A short window of time when they were together and she wasn't bound by the professional constraints of working with him.

Gabriel had his own set path, and Clara couldn't deviate from hers. That would mean chaos, and she didn't do chaos. A good job, a secure home and a heart that couldn't be broken was what she did. But maybe they could emulate the glorious sunset that was beginning to fill the sky. A blaze of colour before the darkness.

'Goodbye, sun…' She curled her hand into a wave, and Gabriel chuckled.

'We'll miss you,' he called across towards the horizon, and then turned suddenly towards Clara. 'I'll miss *you…*'

'I'll miss you too.' She could admit it now.

'But the sun's not quite down yet.' His lips twitched into a smile.

'No, it isn't.'

Gabriel was perfectly capable of starting an affair, letting it runs its course, and then ending it within the space of a few days. Clara trusted that he would play by those rules and that he wouldn't hurt her. He'd let her go and she'd return to work next week. The thought of how it might feel to touch him, and have him touch her, made it all seem possible.

When she turned, looking back at the house, she saw that the group on the veranda was starting to break up. Leo had risen from his seat, and was walking towards the large garage, presumably about to take their guests home.

'I should say goodbye,' Gabriel said quietly. Clearly he felt awkward with the women who had lost their sons when he had survived.

'Go. I'll stay here and appreciate the science.'

Maybe Gabriel would take the opportunity of speaking to his father when he returned. As she watched him walk away from her, up the beach, Clara could only hope that he might.

CHAPTER FIFTEEN

GABRIEL HAD WAITED for his father's return, and then all hell had broken loose. Clara returned from the beach to the sound of raised voices coming from Leo's study.

'Is everything all right?' she asked Alessia, who had met her on the veranda, carrying two glasses of lemonade.

'No. I do not think so.' She put the glasses down on the table and sat down, motioning for Clara to join her. 'Leo tells me that the making of an omelette requires the breaking of eggs.'

Both women jumped as the sound of a door slamming came from the house. Then whoever had walked out on the other obviously returned for a second round, because the sound of voices swelled again.

'I hope they don't break too many.' Clara felt a little guilty now.

'Do you?' Gabriel's mother looked at her thoughtfully. 'I was rather hoping they might break them all.'

* * *

It was a surprise to find that the house wasn't in ruins when Clara awoke the following morning. Gabriel and his father had still been closeted in the study when she'd gone to bed, and the house was suspiciously quiet now.

She showered and dressed, hoping that the sudden peace meant that all the available eggs had now been broken and that some kind of resolution had been reached. But when she went downstairs, she found Alessia alone in the kitchen, drinking coffee.

'Where are they?' If they'd gone to fight a duel at dawn, she doubted that Gabriel's mother would be smiling.

'Gone to the office. I told Leo that if he must shout, he should do it there.' Gabriel's mother got to her feet, pouring a cup of coffee for Clara. 'Do not worry. There is nothing you or I can do.'

'I may have done too much already. I told Gabriel I thought he should talk to his father.' Guilt started to nag at Clara again.

'You did the right thing, this is long overdue. Sit down and eat.'

The day had passed slowly. Clara had spent most of it working, because she couldn't think of anything else to do. At four o'clock she heard Gabriel and his father return, and decided to stay put. She'd already meddled enough.

Half an hour later, the sound of movement came from the sitting room outside her bedroom. Then a loud rap on her bedroom door made her jump.

'Are you coming out?'

Clara opened the door, poking her head around it. 'Has the all-clear sounded yet?'

'I wouldn't go so far as to say that. I'm sorry to be such a bad host…' Gabriel was standing in the middle of the room, his hands in his pockets. He looked surprisingly relaxed, and more than a little handsome.

'Forget that. I think I'm probably the house guest from hell.'

He chuckled. 'No, you're not. Everything you said was entirely right, and I needed to hear it. I needed to hear what Dad had to say as well.'

'Dad?' She narrowed her eyes. 'Is that a good sign? You've worked things out?'

'Not even close. It's going to take a little longer than this.' His gaze dropped to the floor and he seemed suddenly awkward. 'I said I love him, though. And he told me he loves me.'

That sounded like a very good start. 'I'm happy for you, Gabriel.'

He nodded, a smile playing around his lips. 'Could I make things up by taking you to dinner?'

'Don't you want to have dinner here tonight?'

'I said I'd be coming back next weekend. Dad's going to stock up on the eggs for my return.' He shot her a smile. Clearly his mother had repeated her views on eggs and omelettes to him. 'I asked them if they minded, and they said it was the least I could do.'

'All right, then. Smart or casual?'

'I'm thinking about a little place I know a little way along the coast. It's right on the beach so you might like to get a little sand between your toes. Forget about blending in, though, you were never very good at that.'

The look on his face told her that it was a compliment, although Clara wasn't sure how. 'Are you telling me that I'm no good at my job?'

'I'm telling you that you're far too beautiful to blend in, Clara.' His gaze held hers for a moment in a frisson of warmth. Then he turned, walking into his bedroom to get changed.

* * *

By coincidence, they both wore white. When he led her out of the house, opening the passenger door of a small, open-topped sports car, Clara felt as if she were entering another world. One where she could pretend, for just an evening, that she was the kind of woman who belonged on the arm of someone like Gabriel.

The restaurant was set on a stretch of private beach, with large tables, beautifully arranged and placed far enough apart to ensure privacy. It served the best food and the best wines, with no waiters eager to reclaim the table as soon as you'd finished your coffee. Gabriel was well known here, and addressed most of the staff by name.

But although it seemed unlikely that she was the first woman he'd brought here, Gabriel made her feel special. Listening to her as if she was the only person under the stars that glimmered above their heads. His dark eyes seemed only for her tonight.

'Thank you, Gabriel. It was a wonderful evening.' The house was quiet when they arrived back, Alessia and Leo obviously having decided on an early night, and Gabriel led her up the steps to the balcony and unlocked the French windows.

'Would you like a nightcap? Or shall we say goodnight?'

This was the one and only night they'd have this opportunity. Tomorrow they'd be going back to London, and she and Gabriel would go their separate ways.

'I…don't want to say goodnight.' Not now. Not until tomorrow.

His eyes darkened suddenly as he took a step towards her. 'I promised you that I wouldn't make a pass at you if you came here with me. It's taken an impressive amount of willpower on my part.'

'And on mine. But I don't work for your family any more. Would it be all right if I made a pass at you?'

'It would be a lot better than just all right…'

She wound her arms around his neck, kissing him. His body responded as if she'd pressed a switch, hardening against hers as he kissed her. Clara tugged at his shirt, tearing it open and pulling it from his shoulders.

'Wait…wait.' He groaned as she ran her tongue across his nipple, drawing back from her. 'After a month of foreplay, perhaps we should take it a little slower.'

'You think so?'

Suddenly he laughed. 'We've both waited long enough.' He picked her up, carrying her through to his bedroom.

They undressed each other, their fingers trembling. It wasn't easy to give Clara the kind of attention she deserved. Seeing her naked, her body strong and yet slim, almost made him come right there and then. When he laid her down on the bed, his fingers brushing her breasts, her body arched as if he was already inside her. He somehow remembered to open the drawer of the bedside cabinet, fumbling with the condom, before she whispered to him that she couldn't wait any longer.

He kissed her, smoothing her hair out on the pillow around her head. It felt dizzyingly wonderful to be inside her at last, as if the piece that the cave had ripped out of his soul had been filled and he was finally whole again.

She stilled suddenly, staring up into his eyes. They'd reached the eye of the storm, desire whirling around them, leaving each small movement enough to render them both breathless.

'Clara…' Her name sounded so sweet on his lips. The realisation that it was the only one he ever wanted to speak hit Gabriel hard.

'This moment, Gabriel.'

He understood. One moment that could never be repeated, but which would last for ever. Unchanging and exquisite.

'This moment…'

Gabriel flexed his hips, and they gasped together. She wrapped her legs around his waist, taking him further inside. The storm took hold of them again and after just a few minutes of the most intense pleasure that Gabriel had ever experienced, he felt her start to come, and he was pushed over the edge with a force that almost made him black out.

Long moments of almost head-splitting release gave way to a breathless embrace. Her body was warm in his arms, and he already wanted to make love to her again. Clara nestled against him, and he kissed her.

'That was…' There wasn't any point in trying to find the words. They simply didn't exist.

'Yes, it was. It *definitely* was.'

'Do you want to sleep?' He drew a sheet up around her shoulders.

'No. You?'

'Not for one moment. We have so much more left to do.'

They'd talked for a while, snuggling together in the darkness. And then Gabriel had made love to her again. This time, he'd taken his time about it.

He wanted to explore every part of her body, demanding that she do whatever she wanted with his. And there was so much that she wanted to do. They whiled away the long hours of the night together, giving and taking everything.

'I suppose it's time…' A spectacular dawn had tinted the sky with red. Clara wondered whether it might be just for them, and whether everyone else saw just a normal sunrise. It seemed possible.

'Yes. How long will it take for you to get packed?'

'Half an hour.'

'I'll raise you on that and meet you in the shower in twenty-five minutes.' He trailed kisses across her cheek.

An extra five minutes with Gabriel was worth

any number of creases in her clothes. Clara got out of bed, blowing him a kiss as she danced through to her own room.

Gabriel had flipped the switch on the shower, turning warm water to cold, and she'd jumped out from under the icy jet with a squeal. That had woken them both up, and Clara felt alert enough to face his parents at the breakfast table. When they left, his mother hugged her warmly, telling her that if she didn't return she'd come to England to find her. And Clara noticed that the handshake between Gabriel and his father turned into a hug.

They sat in the back seat of the car together, without touching. The driver was probably discreet enough not to mention anything he saw in his rear-view mirror, but Gabriel seemed to know instinctively that Clara was more comfortable with keeping their relationship to themselves. It was only when they'd settled into their seats on the private plane, and the stewardess had gone to her own seat for take-off, that his hand moved towards her.

'You're tired.' His finger grazed her chin.

'Would you like to come home with me and… sleep a little?'

'Sleep? You're seriously asking me to come home with you and sleep?'

'It's the weekend. We can improvise.' He leaned forward, whispering into her ear, 'We could sleep all day and make love all night if we wanted.'

That irresistible smile of his turned improvisation into a plan. It turned leaving, because Clara knew that was what she had to do, into staying for just a little longer.

'Sounds perfect. Do you have any strawberries?'

'We can stop for some on the way…'

Gabriel could see that Clara *was* tired. She'd slept a little on the plane, and when the car delivered them back to his house, she left her luggage untouched in the hallway and followed him upstairs. London was as hot as Italy at the moment, or at least the crowded streets made it seem so, and they stripped off their clothes and curled up on the bed together.

This was a first. He held her as she drifted off

to sleep, and realised that this was exactly what he wanted to do. A dreamless sleep was usually just a natural consequence of sex, but with Clara, Gabriel didn't care whether he dreamt or not. He knew she'd understand the bad dreams and be there for him, and if his dreams were of her then he'd find the way to make them real when she woke up.

The suggestion that sex was a way of connecting, in a world where love was just too complicated, wasn't new to Gabriel. When the realities of a relationship set in, which generally didn't take very long at all, it was time for a civilised goodbye. But Clara was different. She'd been his friend first, through one of the most challenging periods of his life. When they'd finally made love it had been more explosive than anything Gabriel might have anticipated.

He didn't even want to make love with her right now. He wanted to sleep with her, then wake her with coffee and strawberry crêpes. He wanted to argue with her and yet know all the while she'd be there to catch him when he fell. To catch her when she fell. He wanted a lazy afternoon, sitting beneath a flapping parasol of a café, watching the world go by, and to dance with her at midnight, surrounded by the lights of the city.

And then he wanted to lie down with her, and give her not just his body but his heart and soul. Gabriel had reckoned that he knew a thing or two about sex, but he'd been wrong. He wanted Clara to teach him what making love was really all about.

On Sunday morning, Gabriel woke in a bed that was creased and crumpled from the night before. Clara wasn't there.

Making coffee maybe. He listened for sounds of her moving around downstairs and heard nothing. She must be making coffee quietly.

The weekend had been perfect. If it hadn't convinced Clara that planning wasn't always a useful guide in life, then nothing would. Neither of them could possibly have planned the moments they'd shared together, and he knew that Clara had felt it too.

He rolled over, and something crunched against his cheek. When he opened his eyes again, he saw that it was a sheet of paper, left on the pillow beside him. Unfolding it, he saw Clara's handwriting.

No goodbyes. Just memories.
Thank you for all of them.
Xox

What?

Gabriel sat up and read the note again. It started off promisingly enough, the *no goodbyes* part was exactly what he'd been intending to say to Clara this morning. The *just memories* shattered all of that, though. He'd been hoping that maybe they could have a little more than memories. That they might take the first tentative steps into exploring some kind of future together.

It would be a bold move on Gabriel's part. Any kind of permanence in a relationship was entirely new to him, and Clara had made it clear that it was territory that she was uneasy about returning to. But bold moves held the possibility of golden results.

And failure. Gabriel threw the note to one side and flopped back onto the pillows. The cry of frustration that escaped his lips failed to make him feel any better. Clara just couldn't do it. She couldn't leave her own past behind and gamble on a future with him.

But he could do it. He could throw the dice again and win her back, because it was the only thing that made any sense to him. And if he was to improve the odds of Clara changing her mind, he needed a plan…

CHAPTER SIXTEEN

CLARA SAT ON the weather-beaten boards of the veranda, fiddling with the motor that she'd just extracted from the back of the refrigerator. The only thing she'd managed to achieve was to get grease all over her hands. The wretched thing wasn't going to be persuaded to work, and she doubted she'd be able to find anywhere that sold spare parts for a model this old.

It had seemed like a good idea at the time. That was the story of her life at the moment. She'd left Gabriel's bed, knowing that she couldn't say goodbye to him, and that it was inevitable that she would have to. Clara couldn't bring herself to trust and he couldn't bring himself to commit. It was a double whammy.

After a day spent crying, she'd dried her eyes and gone back to work. Her next project had been a straightforward one, and had given her time to think about the idea that Gabriel had planted in her head.

She wanted something more than this. She'd gone to her boss, telling him that she was thinking of going back into medicine.

He'd told her that he didn't want to lose her, but that he'd support whatever decision she made. Security work was all or nothing, and there was no room for the half-hearted. And in an act of genuine kindness, which had touched Clara's heart, he'd offered to contact a friend of his who had a holiday place in Mexico. It had no mod cons, but it was situated on a safe, secluded beach and offered the chance to be alone and think. If Clara could do without Wi-Fi and a phone signal for a couple of weeks, he'd make the call.

No Wi-Fi, and the certain knowledge that her phone wasn't about to ring sounded like the height of luxury. And the decision that she'd agonised over seemed so much simpler. Medicine was the career she really wanted, and she was going to make the change. It left her even more time to think about Gabriel. To miss him in the night. To tell herself every day that she might go back and restart her career, but that there was no going back where Gabriel was concerned.

And now the fridge was broken. So much for the joys of solitude.

An SUV, covered in dust, turned off the road and wound its way along the track towards the house. Someone must be lost. It drew to a halt and the driver got out. Dark hair and golden skin, his eyes hidden behind a pair of sunglasses. Pale chinos and a white casual shirt, sweat stains on the back from a long drive. Gabriel.

Clara put her hand up to shade her eyes, hoping that it would hide the tears. Why did he have to come here? More to the point, *how* had he found out where she was?

'You weren't easy to find.' Gabriel's habit of getting to the point pre-empted her first question.

'How did you?'

'I called you and I couldn't get an answer. So I contacted your boss, and he said that you were on holiday. I asked him if you were going anywhere nice.'

'In other words, you used your position as a client to get the information out of him.'

Gabriel nodded. 'Yes, I did. I'm hoping you might forgive me for that.'

She'd forgive him anything, but she still wished he hadn't done it. If Gabriel wanted to indulge in emotional risk-taking it was up to him. She preferred not to.

'And so you came all the way to Mexico. Couldn't it have waited until I got home?'

'Probably. But you know I can't resist a grand gesture.' He took off his sunglasses, and the look in his eyes belied the joke. Gabriel was deadly serious.

'I'm not in the mood for any grand gestures, Gabriel. All I want at the moment is to get this to work.' She picked up the motor. 'Since I've just taken this out of the refrigerator, you'll understand that I can't offer you a cold beer.'

He grinned. 'Warm will be fine.'

Clara got to her feet, walking into the kitchen. Why had she mentioned beer? But now that she had, she could do with one herself. The length of time that it took to drink it would be a convenient measure for the time she'd give Gabriel to say whatever he had to, before she sent him on his way again.

The beer turned out to be reasonably cool still, and she handed him a bottle, sitting down next to him. Levering the cap off hers, she passed him the bottle opener. He flipped off the cap, tipping his bottle towards hers.

'Cheers.'

'What did you come for, Gabriel? It wasn't the

beer.' He seemed different. More assured, as if he'd found his place in the world, and liked it a lot better than the one he'd inhabited before.

'I've been talking to my father. He's changed his mind about my taking the company over when he retires.'

'What?' Clara started guiltily. 'He's disinheriting you?'

Gabriel chuckled. 'Yeah, I suppose he is, really. By agreement, though. I told him how I felt and he told me that I was an idiot. I accused him of not listening and we both thumped the table for a while. We've decided that having a board of directors appoint a CEO is a perfectly good way forward.'

Clara couldn't help grinning. 'So you worked it out.'

'Yes. I dare say there will be a bit of shouting before we manage to fine-tune all the details, but my mother's relieved that the door slamming is now a thing of the past. I've been seeing a counsellor too, to talk about trauma issues.'

He was serious about this. Gabriel wanted to change and he didn't do anything by halves.

'That's good, Gabriel. Really good.'

'I stumble every day. I've fallen flat on my face a few times...'

'I know you can make it.' Sweat trickled down her spine. The realisation that Gabriel was turning into the kind of man who might be able to offer love, but that it was too late for him to offer it to her, made her want to cry.

'I have a plan.'

'You? A plan?' Clara almost choked on her beer.

He shot her a reproving look. 'I don't know how this thing with my father is going to turn out, or quite what's going to emerge from my counselling. Everything could change, or nothing.'

That sounded a bit less as if Gabriel had undergone a personality transplant. 'So the plan is to go with the flow?'

'No. The plan is to love you. Truly and unfailingly, whatever else happens. I don't ask anything of you, other than that you try to love me, but before you give your answer, you should know what you're taking on.'

His hand was trembling now. Gabriel was the bravest person she knew, and capable of taking the boldest of steps, but this had the power to break him.

Clara took a deep breath. She believed him. He'd always been true to his word.

'I…love you too.'

'You do?' He seemed almost surprised.

'I loved you from the moment I saw you. I just couldn't trust enough to take a chance on you. And I was wrong.'

'Then you'll stay with me? Take whatever life gives us?'

'Yes.' Clara flung her arms around his neck, hanging on tight. 'Come inside. The water for the shower has to be pumped, and it never gets very hot. And there's an old brass bedstead, which creaks.'

'Perfect.' He lifted her up and she wound her legs around his waist. It was impossible to even think about letting him go. Because Gabriel, the man who could give her anything she wanted, had given her the one thing she'd thought she could never have. He'd given her his heart.

EPILOGUE

One week later

DURING THE LAST week they'd never strayed far enough from each other that Clara couldn't reach out and touch Gabriel. They'd walked two miles to the village each day to buy food, which was cooked on the barbecue on the veranda. It was like being shipwrecked together, and being with Gabriel made it seem as if she'd been washed up in Paradise.

But it had to end sometime. Urgent business, which couldn't be postponed, had taken Gabriel away from her today. He'd promised to miss her for every moment they were apart, and as the sun went down Clara sat on the porch, looking for the plume of dust that meant his car was approaching.

Finally he came. Smiling as he walked towards her, and taking her in his arms for a hug so tight that they might have been separated for much longer than a day.

'I've got some champagne in the car. Chilling…'

'That sounds wonderful. You didn't get *that* in the village, did you?'

'I stopped at a wine bar thirty miles along the coast. They were good enough to throw in some ice and a bucket along with the champagne. I drove as quickly as I could.'

'I'd better get some glasses, then.' Clara laughed, running up the steps to the veranda and into the kitchen. Champagne on the beach, at sunset, with the man she loved sounded perfect. Even if it was drunk from a couple of tumblers that didn't match.

Gabriel poured the champagne, and they strolled arm in arm down to the water's edge, kicking off their shoes and walking in the surf.

'So how was your day? Did you get everything you wanted to do done?'

'Not quite.' He frowned, suddenly uncertain. That wasn't like Gabriel at all…

He bent down, propping the champagne bottle upright in the sand. Then he wrapped his arms around her shoulders, his brow creasing with anxiety.

Clara reached up and kissed him. ‘What is it? Do we have to go home?’

‘Not yet.’ He took a deep breath. ‘Would you marry me, Clara?’

That was the last thing she was expecting him to say. And they’d talked about this already. She’d told him that his love was the only reassurance that she needed.

‘Gabriel…no.’ Her throat seemed to close, as if her heart was trying to stop the words from getting out. ‘If this is your way of showing me that you won’t leave, it’s not necessary. I don’t want you to feel under any pressure to rush into anything.’

The look in his eyes silenced Clara. It was the Gabriel she knew, the one who knew what he wanted and would reach for it despite the risk. He fell to one knee in front of her, holding her hands between his.

‘I messed that up. Call it beginner’s nerves. I’m going to give it another go… Clara Holt, I know you love me and I love you too. The only thing that could possibly make me happier than I am now is if you’ll agree to marry me.’

This was real. Clara reached for him, trying to pull him close, but he stayed stubbornly on his knees. 'Yes, Gabriel. I'll marry you, of course I will.' She fell into his arms, kissing him as the surf washed around them.

'I have a ring…' He reached into his pocket.

'Is *that* what you were doing today? I thought you had business with your father's company.'

He shook his head, grinning. 'I said urgent business. I don't believe I ever mentioned my father's company. And this is extremely urgent.'

When Clara held out her hand, it was shaking. He kissed her finger, before carefully sliding the ring onto it. A single, square-cut diamond flashed in the dying rays of the sun.

'It's beautiful, Gabriel. Thank you so much, for everything. For coming here to find me and for loving me and asking me to marry you…' Tears welled in Clara's eyes.

'I should be thanking you. For being the love of my life, and for saying yes.'

Sleep could wait. They'd danced on the beach together to the soft music of the waves, moonlight guiding their way back to the house. Making plans and making love until the sun rose.

'When?' Gabriel had already asked where and Clara had suggested Italy.

'Soon.' She kissed him. 'Although I suppose it might take some time to organise everything…'

'All we really need is you and me.' Gabriel traced his finger slowly along her shoulder. 'How about next week? We'd have to go to Vegas. We can't get a licence that quickly in Italy.'

'Seriously?'

'Why not?' He pulled her hand to his lips, kissing it. 'I don't want to wait, Clara.'

'I don't want to wait either.' Clara decided that there was just one thing she was going to insist on. 'I don't want to be married by an Elvis impersonator, though.'

Gabriel chuckled. 'No, that wasn't what I had in mind. The Grand Canyon's less than an hour away by helicopter…'

Clara caught her breath. 'We can get married in the Grand Canyon. *Next week!* But what about your parents?'

'When I called to give them our news, I asked my mother if she'd be disappointed if we did our own thing for the wedding. She told me that as long as she can throw us a big party when we get back, she'll be happy. What do you think?'

His smile dared her to say yes. This was the way it was going to be from now on, Gabriel challenging the impossible and turning it into something real and exciting. It was a journey that Clara couldn't wait to make.

'I think… Vegas, here we come.'

* * * * *